DYING TO MEET

DYING TO MEET

Girvani Dhyani

B L O O M S B U R Y
LONDON • OXFORD • NEW YORK • NEW DELHI • SYDNEY

BLOOMSBURY INDIA
Bloomsbury Publishing India Pvt. Ltd
Second Floor, LSC Building No. 4, DDA Complex, Pocket C – 6 & 7,
Vasant Kunj, New Delhi 110070

BLOOMSBURY, BLOOMSBURY INDIA and the Diana logo
are trademarks of Bloomsbury Publishing Plc

First published in India 2024
This edition published 2024

ISBN: PB: 978-93-54352-15-7; e-ISBN: 978-93-54353-68-0
2 4 6 8 10 9 7 5 3 1

Typeset in Fournier MT Std by Manipal Technologies Limited
Printed and bound in India by Thomson Press India Ltd

MIX
Paper | Supporting responsible forestry
FSC® C010615
www.fsc.org

PART I

ALL THAT GLITTERS IS NOT GOLD

I

I was at JFK Airport, waiting to board my flight. I looked at the books I had picked up from the Hudson news stand. The airport somehow always had the best selection of books, which is why every time I travelled, I made it a point to arrive a little early so I could browse around and pick up some good reading material for the long flight from New York to New Delhi.

I looked at my watch—it was still an hour before boarding. I opened my Ziploc to check whether or not my stash of sleep aids—Zzzquil, Unisom, melatonin, etc.—was there. It was. I was all set. The thing about sleep aids is that they need to be perfectly timed for them to kick in at the right time. I had a fear of flying and if it wasn't for so special an occasion, I would never have mustered up the courage to fly down to Delhi. My hands were getting clammy; I wiped them on my pants.

I walked past the duty-free shops and, for a moment, was tempted to go inside and buy myself a carton of Marlboro Lights and candy, but I was trying to quit smoking and lose weight, so I instead made my way to the Air India lounge. Inside were uncles guzzling down double Black Labels before boarding the same nonstop fourteen-hour flight to Delhi as me. Children were running around, filling their plates with the bland food laid out at the buffet. An elderly lady couldn't keep her eyes off me. She seemed as if she was itching to chat with me and possibly find out every tiny detail about my life. I just hoped the nosy aunty and I wouldn't be seated next to each other on the flight. I noticed a girl around twelve years of age looking at me very intently. I smiled at her but she didn't smile back and shifted her glance towards my hands instead. I noticed I had inadvertently been picking on my cuticles and now they were bleeding. It was a habit I had picked up, which I abstained from only when I started getting gel manicures on the regular. But for some reason, when I got nervous, I started doing it again. It was a tick I had.

I headed towards the restroom. I was wearing a beige trench coat, so when I quickly stuffed my hands in my pocket, they left a bloody streak. I went straight to the washbasin and turned on the hot water. I closed my eyes in pain as the hot water stung. Why was a trip that was supposed to be fun, causing me so much anxiety? I dried off my hands and pulled out a vitamin cuticle gel to coat my cuticles and thanked my Guatemalan nail salon lady, Gilda, who had insisted I took some with me.

I had lived in the United States since I was nine years old and so it was the only life I had ever known. This was my first trip back to India in several years, and the main reason I was going back was to have a reunion with my friends, whom I hadn't seen in ten years. At first, I wasn't sure if I would be able to take time off work. But it was Riya's fortieth birthday and she was very keen to have us all there to celebrate with an all-girls fun weekend in Gurugram, near New Delhi. There was no way I was going to miss her birthday. So I moved a few things around on my calendar and here I was, waiting to board my flight.

Thinking about my friends brought a smile to my face. We were a group of four, including me. Sameera Khan, Naina Kumari and I had met at New York University (NYU), where Naina and I were pursuing our master's in law (LLM) and Sameera—or Sam, as we liked to call her—was doing a master's in international relations. Riya Sharma was a couple of years older than us, and we just happened to meet her on one of our late-night outings to Kathi Roll Factory in West Village. Over copious amounts of masala chai, we all became friends for life almost overnight. I had been in touch with Sam and Riya on and off over the years, but we hadn't met in person in five years. Naina, however, had altogether disappeared from the face of the earth. We had all last seen her almost ten years ago when we graduated. I couldn't help but wonder if she would make it to Riya's fortieth. The plans for this weekend were made over several weeks on our email group, and even though Naina's old uni email was part of the chain, we had gotten no response from her—none of us had any idea whether or not she was even aware of Riya's party, let alone if she would come.

My thoughts were interrupted by an announcement for my flight. I picked up my overnight bag. Since I was going to be in Delhi only for a couple of days, I had decided to travel super light, so I didn't bother with a check-in bag. I looked at my Tumi bag and saw the initials 'MSG', for Maya Singh Gondal—my married name. I now went by Maya Singh, ever since our divorce, but my bag was a gift from my ex-husband and still carried my old initials. I couldn't be bothered with changing it; the marriage had been short-lived, lasting all of two months before I realised what a scoundrel he was. I had learnt my lesson. No more impulsive Vegas-style elopements. 'The weasel', as I liked to refer to him, had been a colleague at my previous law firm. Except I realised what he was really like only after we got married. Almost four years had elapsed now since the divorce and the thought of him still made me want to retch. I had always thought the foundation of any relationship should be friendship. But what I didn't know was that people could be very different behind closed doors. The weasel was controlling to the point of being oppressive. If I got home from work before him, he scanned the entire house for clues suspecting that I had been with someone else in his absence; and if that wasn't enough, he would go through the trash cans, too, looking for evidence. Initially, I thought it was kind of cute that he was so possessive, but soon, I realised it was more like a sickness. In retrospect, it wasn't the divorce that hurt but the humiliation of a failed marriage and that I had been a bad judge of character. This was another reason why I hadn't seen the girls in so long. But now so much time had elapsed, I just needed a break to let my hair down and connect with old friends.

I entered the plane and took my seat, and accepted my welcome drink. Putting on my wireless noise-cancelling headphones, I played a Moby song and closed my eyes. At some point, I drifted off to sleep and didn't notice that another person had come and sat next to me. When I woke up, I noticed it was Dhruv Khanna, an old friend from NYU. Talk about coincidence! I had had a feeling this weekend was going to be full of nostalgia.

'Oh my goodness! I can't believe it. Dhruv, is that really you?'

'Sure is. How have you been, Maya? I was waiting for you to wake up. I swapped seats with the lady over there so I could sit with you,' he said, smiling, pointing to the aunty I had seen at the lounge. Thank God for small mercies.

'Well, this is a pleasant surprise. I haven't seen you in ages.'

'Yes, it has been a while. How have you been?'

'I'm doing very well, thanks. I work as an immigration attorney in the city. So work's been keeping me busy. What about you? Last I heard, you had moved back to India.'

'Yup, back in India. I work as a consultant but I'm involved in projects that keep bringing me back to New York every other month.'

'Well, call me next time you're in town so we can catch up. I'll take you to some of the cool dive bars in the city.'

'Will do. How are the others doing? Riya, Sam, Naina? What's up with them?'

'Actually, I am going to Delhi to meet the girls. It's Riya's fortieth birthday this weekend,' I said.

'Time sure does fly. Riya is forty?! Wow. That's great! Gosh, I still remember those fun days at NYU. You girls were crazy,' Dhruv said, laughing.

'Those indeed were the days,' I said wistfully.

'I still remember the cook-ins we had at your apartment. With the suspicious-looking Jell-O shots that Rishi Sinha prepared.'

'Don't forget the night we got completely hammered and decided to make lasagna at two in the morning. We ended up burning it and the smoke alarm went off and we were in complete denial and insisted the neighbours had set it off, remember? Things only registered when the fire department showed up and gave us a stern warning.'

'Yes, I do remember that night. By the way, how is Naina now?' he asked.

'Unfortunately, I haven't been in touch with her. I have no idea,' I said.

'Well, okay. I was wondering how she was doing, especially after what happened the last time we met.'

'What happened?'

'Don't you know?'

'Know what?'

'Well, it was 4 a.m. on the day of our graduation. I was living alone in a studio apartment at the time. I heard a knock on the door and it was Naina. She looked pretty distraught, and since it had been raining, she was completely drenched. She came inside and explained that she needed a place to crash. Something about family problems and how she needed some time alone. She made me promise that I wouldn't tell anyone where she was, especially you. I didn't push her. She looked like she had been crying for hours. Without saying another word, she took to the couch and went off to sleep.'

'Then what happened?'

'Well, I got dressed the next morning and came to attend the graduation ceremony with the rest of you. I asked her if she wanted a ride. She refused, saying she would meet me there directly. When I returned in the evening, I saw her sprawled on the ground with an empty bottle of sleeping pills lying next to her. I called 911 in a panic and they rushed her to the hospital, where they were able to pump her stomach in the nick of time. I had to leave the hospital for an urgent meeting. When I returned to the hospital, Naina wasn't there.'

'What do you mean? Where did she go?' I was shocked at what I was hearing.

'I don't know. She didn't call me or leave a note. I tried her cell phone number, but it was switched off. I have no idea where she went.'

'Why didn't you reach out to me or one of the others?'

'I had a flight to catch later that night but I did try your number, Maya. I couldn't get through.'

I knew why Dhruv was unable to reach me that night. After Naina's no-show at graduation, I remember bidding farewell to Riya and Sam and getting on the E train and riding to the last stop. I had felt this overwhelming need to be alone. Naina and I were best friends. We had waited for this day for so long and when the time had come to walk across that stage—the culmination of all our hard work—there was no sign of her anywhere. Her absence seemed like a grim foreshadowing of a forever rift in our friendship.

But Dhruv's revelation had shed new light on that day. I was devastated to think of Naina going through so much pain alone. 'I had no idea all this had happened ... I don't understand why Naina would try to take her own life.'

'I tried reaching out to Naina repeatedly after that, but she never responded,' Dhruv said sadly.

'Have you been in touch with her at all over the years?'

'No, I haven't. It's like she just ghosted everyone.'

This conversation was making me sick. I excused myself and rushed to the aeroplane toilet. I threw up violently. I stood in front of the mirror for a couple of minutes, trying to gather myself. Dhruv's account of our graduation day came as a complete shock to me. I splashed some water on my face. I needed to compose myself. It was a long flight and the last thing I needed right now was a panic attack. I pulled out a sleeping pill and slipped it in my mouth. I then decided I needed a stronger dose and popped another one. My hands were shaking.

I had lied about last seeing Naina around graduation. I had seen her once again, about five years ago—the last time all of us had been together. Riya had come to New York for an appointment with a high-profile fertility doctor. She had invited me to a Bon Jovi concert. Unfortunately, Sam was in London so it was just going to be Riya and me. She'd gone all out and had Yug, her husband, book us a suite at Madison Square Garden. We had all got dressed to the nines and even though nobody really listened to Bon Jovi any longer, the experience of attending a live concert at one of the world's most famous arenas had been electrifying. From the suite, we could enter the concert arena and grab any random seat.

Other than people's cell phone flashlights swaying to the music, the concert hall had been in complete darkness. As I had scanned the area around us, I'd felt a pair of eyes looking directly at me. Those eyes had belonged to Naina. There had been a partition dividing our section from hers. I'd have had to climb over two rows to get to the divider. I had promptly started making my way towards her, but when she had realised this, she had turned around and started heading towards the exit. I had tried to call out to her, but I bet she couldn't hear me. By the time I had reached the divider, Naina had left. Had I just imagined her being there? We had been drinking for a couple of hours before then… There was no way she didn't know we were going to the concert too, since Riya posted about everything on social media. I had spotted a piece of paper on the floor where Naina had stood and asked somebody to pass it to me.

It had said 'Penn Station'—unmistakably in Naina's handwriting.

I heard somebody knock gently on the aeroplane bathroom door. I looked at my watch; I had been inside for fifteen minutes now. I dried my eyes and returned to my seat.

'Are you okay, Maya? I didn't mean to upset you. I am really sorry.'

'I guess just hearing about Naina upset me. All the memories and the time that we spent together just came rushing back.'

'I know you guys had always been very close. I didn't mean to gossip, but I was honestly concerned about her well-being and just wanted to know how she was doing, even though it has been several years.'

'I know, Dhruv. You always did have a soft corner for her, didn't you?' I said teasingly. He blushed. I was seeing Dhruv after a long time, and the last thing I wanted was for him to feel awkward around me, and that too onboard a fourteen-hour flight. He had just been concerned about Naina.

I had second thoughts about attending the reunion now that Dhruv had shared this new information with me, but I really wanted to meet everyone.

'Do you mind if I sleep off? I've had a hectic week at work.' My energy was quickly draining and I just wanted to drift off.

'Sure.'

I closed my eyes and put on my headphones. The sleeping pills were finally kicking in. The stewardess and Dhruv tried to wake me up for mealtimes, but I brushed them off and continued to sleep. I only woke up once we landed in Delhi. I made small talk with Dhruv as he headed towards the baggage belts. We parted ways, promising to keep in touch before I walked towards the exit.

'Maya!'

I heard Dhruv call out to me. I looked around. I checked to see if I had all my bags and belongings with me. I didn't think I'd left anything behind. I turned around and he jogged over to me.

'Maya, there is something else I forgot to mention to you about the Naina incident. When I returned to the hospital that day and she was missing, I spoke to a nurse to find out if she knew where Naina had disappeared. Since she had been admitted for attempting suicide, there was no way they were going to let her just walk out of the hospital. The nurse on duty told me that a man had visited her while I was away. She suspected Naina left with him before the hospital staff could detain her on a seventy-two-hour psychiatric hold. When I asked the nurse for more details about the visitor, she couldn't tell me much. But I hope this is helpful.'

'Thanks, it does help.' I gave Dhruv a quick hug and made my way to the exit.

I saw somebody holding up an iPad with my name on it. Riya had sent someone to pick me up despite my telling her I would be able to reach her place by myself. She was always so thoughtful. I made my way towards the canary yellow SUV parked outside in waiting and smiled. That's so Riya. I was really looking forward to spending the weekend with my girls, especially after hearing what Dhruv had to say.

2

The drive to Gurugram from the airport was smooth. There was barely any traffic now, thanks to all the underpasses that had been built in the last couple of years, according to the driver. This was a lot quicker and easier drive than the one I had to make to get to JFK from my office in Manhattan.

This was my first time in Gurugram and I had heard so much about the city. It did not disappoint. I could see malls, restaurants, movie theatres, glitzy high-rises, and just as I started marvelling at how great the roads and highways were, the driver took an exit which brought us to a road under construction. I was a little uneasy with the sudden change in route. Thankfully, he guessed what I was thinking.

'Madam, this is the way to Riya Madam's house.'

'She lives here?' I was a little taken aback, looking outside the window and seeing barren land, a sudden departure from the opulence I had just witnessed a couple of minutes ago.

'Yes, Madam. Is this your first time in India?'

'No, I have been here before. Why do you ask?' I was on a secluded road with a driver I barely knew, so I thought it best to keep my answers curt.

'There is a lot of new construction and development going on in Gurugram. You will see in the next six months, this very road will have been paved over and smoothed. These barren lands that you are seeing around you will be filled with trees and greenery and new apartment buildings.'

'Okay. But this does seem to be a little out of the way.'

'Madam, the rich are like that. They thrive on exclusivity and privacy. Did you know the nearest hospital is at least 7 kilometres away? The police station is even further away. Till about a year ago, there were only villages all around. But with all this new construction, the villagers have relocated to other parts of the city.'

'Don't you ever get scared driving down this empty road at night?'

'Madam, we are used to it. Besides…' The driver leaned over and opened the glove compartment—there was a gun inside.

'This is for not just my own safety but yours, too, Madam.'

The sight of the gun shocked me. It was a common sight in certain parts of the US, but I thought India had stricter laws. I avoided making eye contact with the driver in the rear-view mirror and instead stared at my phone to indicate that the conversation was over. But I guess he didn't quite get the hint.

'Madam, you asked how I know so much about real estate. I used to work for a local real estate company as a driver. The company went bust due to fraudulent deals and I lost my job. Thankfully, I found employment with Yug Sir, who is the kindest man I know. I hope to serve him for life.'

We finally reached our destination—a shiny new ten-storey apartment building. I noticed that most of the units were not occupied—there were no blinds or curtains in the windows, and some balconies were still being worked on. There was scaffolding all along the building, and I could see a construction worker hanging off a rope with only a harness to support him, cleaning a window on the ninth floor. I looked around and saw an excavator and some construction workers digging up what looked like a swimming pool. Ahead of us, some sort of a clubhouse was being built. A sign indicated the future clubhouse would contain a spa, restaurant and gym. But it looked like it would take several months before any of these things came into existence, let alone become operational.

'Madam, don't worry about the construction workers. They leave by 5 p.m. so there will be no noise to disturb you until at least 8 a.m. the next morning. But given the weather forecast, these guys probably won't be back for the next couple of days. There is a big storm expected.'

The news of an approaching storm and the sight of the secluded construction site sent a shiver up my spine, but I tried ignoring all negative thoughts and reminded myself why I was here.

'What about you?' I asked out of concern for the driver.

'Madam, I have school-going kids. I'll take my scooter and go back to town,' he said, pointing to a white scooter parked in the corner.

I thanked Riya's driver for the ride and stepped out of the car. My phone started buzzing. It was somebody calling from the office. They knew I was on leave and I had told them to call me only if it was urgent. I ignored the call at first, but when my phone kept ringing incessantly, I assumed it must be important enough for them to try and reach me this desperately.

'Yes?' I answered curtly. I hardly ever took leave and so was annoyed at being disturbed. A few days of peace is all I had asked for. I had left on a Thursday and was going to be back in the office on Tuesday morning; yet, whatever it was, it couldn't wait.

'Maya, it's Kiran from the front desk,' the receptionist from my office said.

'Yes, Kiran?'

'An old friend of yours has been desperately trying to reach you. She says she needs to speak with you urgently.'

'Can't it wait? I just landed and I am exhausted. What's her name?'

'Naina Kumari.'

My heart was in my mouth. I hadn't spoken to Naina in years and here she was, calling me just as I was thinking about her today after that conversation with Dhruv.

'Is she on the other line right now?'

'Yes.'

'Can you patch her in please?'

I looked at my watch. I was standing on the porch of Riya's building, looking out at the construction, and my heart was racing. I was excited as well as nervous to talk to Naina. I really did not know what to expect.

'Hello. Is that you, Maya?' Naina whispered.

'Yes, Naina, how are you?' I asked.

'Maya—' Before she could complete her sentence, the phone got disconnected. I wanted to scream. I called the office back. 'Kiran, did my friend leave a number? We seemed to have got disconnected.'

'Hang on a minute, let me look it up. No, sorry, the number was withheld. We just changed our phone lines so I can't trace the call, either.'

'That's fine.'

'How was your flight, Lady M?'

I couldn't help smiling. The joke at the office was that when I was stressed or not in a great mood, a pastry from Lady M, a Japanese confectionery, usually did the trick. Kiran had sensed I was a little stressed.

'Thanks, Kiran. It was hectic and I am quite exhausted.'

'Get some rest, and I promise, no more phone calls. Enjoy your weekend and see you next week!'

I stood for a couple of minutes still reeling from Naina's sudden call after so long. I noticed a petite lady standing in a corner, staring at me. She was wearing an all-black outfit. I noticed her golden pair of ballet flats. An unusual choice of shoes, considering she was in some kind of professional attire. If I didn't know better, it would almost feel like she had been listening in on my conversation. I noticed the driver had already taken my bag upstairs.

'Maya Madam, please follow me,' the lady said.

I was a little taken aback that she knew my name.

'What's your name?'

'My name is Devi. I am the housekeeper.'

I noticed that Devi looked unusually nervous and had broken into a sweat, even though it was a cool, overcast afternoon.

'Are you okay?'

'Yes, thank you. Please follow me.'

Devi took me towards the elevator. She punched in a number on the keypad and pressed the 'PH' button. The elevator doors soon opened into a lobby. Riya lived in the penthouse unit. I asked Devi where Riya was, and she told me Riya had gone shopping with Sam. I was disappointed at having to wait. I asked her if a madam by the name of Naina had also arrived. Devi looked clueless, so I let it pass. I was still trying to figure out why Naina had reached out to me. I made a mental note to ask Riya and Sam if they had heard from her as well.

I unpacked quickly, taking out the bottle of vodka from my bag—the group's favourite liquor. I asked Devi to put it in the freezer. A trick I had learned was that alcohol never froze, except for wine, which contained some amount of water. I went to Riya's living room and looked out of the huge French window. It offered some breathtaking views of the Gurugram skyline. The gathering storm clouds made me nervous, especially since Riya's building seemed to be secluded, with no other settlement in sight for miles. But I brushed away any negative thoughts from my head; I had a bad habit of always looking at the downside. What's the worst that could happen? I'd be marooned in a gorgeous penthouse with girls I loved, reminiscing about the good times we'd shared.

I couldn't help but look back at our friendship and how it all started. We all had difficult lives and scars that we carried even today. I had a very tumultuous childhood, and it had been very difficult for me to open up and get close to anyone. It was for financial reasons that I had decided to stay with Sam and Naina, at first. We were all struggling in New York City and living together just made sense. At first, I did not let any of the girls in. I kept most of our communication confined to the logistics of cohabiting. I left early in the morning while everyone was still asleep and returned late after they had gone to bed. I did not want to talk to anyone. Every time I had allowed anybody to get close to me in the past, they had only hurt me, and I wasn't prepared to let that happen again.

That was until I got a bad case of the flu and became so weak that if it wasn't for Naina and Sam looking after me, I probably wouldn't have survived. That's when the ice finally broke and we became friends for life. Eventually, Riya joined us and our gang was complete.

Initially, after graduation, Riya, Sam and I tried to stay in touch. We would meet at least once a year. But around five years ago, around the time I met the weasel, we lost touch. Until Riya reached out to us, a few months ago.

I was hoping this weekend would change all that and we would stay in touch this time.

The last time we were all under one roof was the night before our graduation. We were sitting in our small apartment drinking rosé out of our coffee mugs and talking about what we thought the future had in store for us. I remember saying that since I was living as an immigrant, I wanted to champion immigrant rights and work hard to be a successful attorney. Sam wanted to work for a non-profit and fight for women's rights. She felt that as a South Asian Muslim woman, a lot of women like her were oppressed and subjected to abuse and didn't have a voice. Riya said she wanted to have a baby and was planning to consult fertility doctors to make it happen as they had already tried everything else. I noticed Naina was quiet, which was unlike her. We had often talked about our goals and aspirations together, since Naina too had studied law. But unlike me, she never wanted to practice. Her circumstances and family had forced her into pursuing law. Naina had been very young when her parents had split. She had gone to live with her mother, who had wanted her to become a doctor or a lawyer, just to put her father and his family down. At the time, I dismissed Naina's silence as insecurity about what the future held for her. Little did I know there was more to it, a lot more.

3

I went into the room arranged for me and noticed there was a pitcher of water and a few cans of La Croix and Diet Coke. Riya was always so thoughtful; she knew exactly what I liked. I turned on my laptop and checked my work email to make sure everything was under control. There was nothing urgent—maybe after my conversation with Kiran earlier, everybody had understood that I was dead serious about not wanting to be disturbed on my vacation. Next, I checked my personal email and noticed that there was still no response from Naina—we still had no idea whether she was coming or not. I decided to drop her a quick line, in case she was still trying to reach me.

I was exhausted, but I knew staying awake was probably the best way to deal with jet lag. I was lying in bed when I noticed a piece of paper being slipped under my door. I went over and picked it up. There was a phone number scribbled on it. I opened my bedroom door to see who had slipped it, but the hallway was empty. I grabbed my cell phone and dialled the number. There was no response. I tried again and it said the number was switched off. I saw the housekeeper standing outside at a distance, dusting a painting that clearly didn't need it. I gestured to her to come to me. She looked a little scared.

'Devi, right?'

'Yes, Madam,' she responded.

'Do you know who slipped this note under my door?'

Devi looked the other way, and I knew it was her.

'Who gave this to you?'

'Ravi at the front gate gave it to me today when I was returning from the vegetable market,' she said.

'Did he say anything else when he handed it over?' I asked.

'He just asked me to give it to the American madam arriving today,' she said.

'Is Ravi at the gate right now?' I asked.

'Yes, he should be there. Would you like me to call him?'

'No, that's fine. I will go talk to him myself.'

I went back to my room and pulled on a sweatshirt and my Uggs. When I went to the elevator, I realised I didn't have the code. I went back in and called out to Devi. She came and punched some numbers in.

'Can you share this code with me? How do I get back in?'

'No, Madam.'

'Excuse me?'

'Madam, I am not allowed to share the code with anybody. When you want to come back upstairs, Ravi will call me from the gate, and I will come downstairs to get you.'

'Okay.' Secretly, I was thinking how ridiculous it was for Devi to have to make multiple trips, but if Riya had rules in place, I knew they had to be respected. Besides, with all the construction workers floating around and given how secluded the area was, it did make sense to have strict security measures in place.

I took the elevator down and made my way to the front gate.

'Ravi?'

'Yes, Madamji,' he said.

'I received this note earlier. Devi gave it to me. Do you know who dropped it off?' I asked, showing him the piece of paper in my hands.

'A lady came earlier this morning and told me to give it to you. Since I can't leave the front gate, I asked Devi to give it to you. Oh yes, she also mentioned that the note should be handed over to nobody else but you. In fact, she insisted.'

'Can you tell me what she looked like?'

'Madamji ... now what can I say?' He said coyly.

'Please, Ravi. Can you describe what this lady looked like? It's important.'

'Well, she was fair, very tall and slim, with long straight hair.'

'Thanks, Ravi,' I said.

I immediately knew it was Naina. She was almost six feet tall, and we'd often teased her about wasting her time studying when she could be walking on ramps as a supermodel. But why was she trying this desperately to reach me now after not having been in touch for so long? Was there something she wanted to share with me in private that she didn't want the others to know? The all-too-familiar feeling of anxiety started taking over me. I needed to compose myself before I went back to Riya's apartment.

Instead of walking towards the main building, I wandered into the grounds and ended up near the under-construction swimming pool. I went and sat down on one of the plastic chairs there and closed my eyes. There was no sign of the sun, and the weather seemed to be turning. The rolling thunderclouds reflected the turmoil I felt within. So many years had gone by and Naina never bothered to check in, and now here she was, desperate to get in touch.

I decided to go back. Ravi must have noticed me walking towards the building and called Devi to come get me, because just as I reached the lobby, the elevator doors opened and there she stood. Walking into the apartment this time, it seemed quieter than before. The strange events of the day, coupled with my jet lag, had drained me. I lay down in bed, hoping to get some sleep.

4

Knock knock!

I opened my eyes and realised I was lying in a pool of sweat. The heating was cranked up and I had passed out without bothering to adjust it. It took me a couple of minutes to find my bearings and realise that the knocking was real.

It was incessant. I slipped on a robe and opened the door, disoriented. It was Riya.

'Hello, hello, sleepyhead,' Riya said as she enveloped me in a warm hug.

'Hey, sorry. I just passed out.'

'No worries. Devi, get Madam some coffee. Black with two sugars.'

I couldn't help but smile. For all of Riya's scatterbrained ways, she had an attention to detail like nobody else I had ever met. Riya followed me inside the room, and I got back under the sheets, propping myself up with pillows. Riya sat down on the only couch in my room. I saw that even just to hang out at home, she had dressed very stylishly. She was wearing a fitted denim jumpsuit with brown booties; her make-up was light, and she wore no jewellery other than a huge solitaire diamond ring, and she was rocking the famous Anna Wintour bob. Only Riya could pull it off.

'It's so good to see you, Riya,' I said.

'Likewise. Turning forty isn't as bad as I thought it would be, because I get to see you girls.'

'Come on, you don't look a year older than thirty.'

'It's all the plastic surgery, Baby. Fillers, Botox, sculpting—you name it.'

'You do realise that as a woman, admitting you went under the knife requires a lot of confidence? By the way, I heard Sam is here already. Where is she? I can't wait to see her!'

'Well, she wanted to visit a few more stores, and I wanted to get back home quickly to see you. She will join us later.'

'What about Naina? Any news?'

'I couldn't reach her, so I don't think she is coming.'

I could see Riya was in an upbeat mood, and I didn't want to ruin her big birthday weekend by telling her about the strange call I received from Naina or the note she had left with the guard, let alone Dhruv's disturbing revelations—especially if she wasn't coming. Even though Riya was a close and dear friend, because she did not attend school with us, she often felt excluded when we talked about common friends or school. This weekend was all about her and I didn't want to detract from that.

'So what's the plan?'

'Well, I had made elaborate plans to spend this weekend at an exclusive, members-only club. I'd booked a private dining room with a tasting menu and a sommelier—the works. But guess what, Mother Nature had other plans. A storm is expected tomorrow night, so we will now be staying in instead. Apparently, there hasn't been a storm like this in the longest time. The construction workers you saw outside won't be coming to work either, which is a blessing in disguise as we won't have to hear the constant sound of machines and hammering. Anyway, enough about my birthday. I am mad at you, Maya. Coming all the way from New York just for a few nights. You should have stayed longer, you know?'

'I know but work has been kind of crazy, and I couldn't miss your fortieth for the world. So I decided I would come at any cost, even if just for a few days.'

'Thanks for coming, my love. Why don't you freshen up and let's grab a bite together. It's almost dinner time and you must be starving. Sam should be here soon.' Riya said.

Riya left the room, and I went to the restroom to freshen up. Devi had brought in a cup of coffee for me. I took a couple of sips and locked my bedroom door. I checked my email to see if Naina had responded. There was no response from her, still.

I was happy to see Riya looking well. I changed into something a little more presentable and joined her in the dining room. I noticed she had a whole array of sushi laid out.

'That looks delicious.'

'It's from Megu—my fave place. Dig in. Sam just got back, too. She's freshening up and will be joining us soon.'

Just then, I saw Sam walk in and was a little taken aback by her appearance. She was wearing a long black burqa. I knew Sam was a religious Muslim, but she had never worn even a headscarf at university, let alone a burqa. I tried not to stare at her and instead went over and hugged her.

'Sam, it's so good to see you,' I said.

'You haven't changed, Maya, even after all these years,' Sam said.

'Girls, I am starving. Can we eat?' Riya said as we settled in.

'Yup,' I said. I grabbed a pair of chopsticks and helped myself to some sashimi. I noticed Sam took a few pieces of edamame and was nibbling on it, while Riya helped herself to spicy tuna rolls.

'I wish Naina was here. I haven't seen her in so many years,' I continued.

I noticed Sam and Riya look at each other; Riya broke into a smile.

'I was hoping to keep this a surprise but guess what? Naina will be joining us tomorrow night,' Riya said.

'What? I can't believe it! After all these years, I will finally get to see her! I didn't want to say anything earlier, but she had called me today. Maybe it was to let me know she would be coming.'

'Yes, that's probably why.' Riya said smilingly.

'Is she staying with us?' I asked.

'Yes, she is. She will be coming tomorrow just in time for dinner and will stay for one night.' Riya said.

'That explains her call. I always felt like there was unfinished business with Naina. I would be glad to have the opportunity to settle it with her, once and for all.'

'Unfinished? Why do you say that?' Sam asked.

'Well, I always found the circumstances under which she vanished from our lives rather odd. She just cut everyone off without saying a word.'

'True, but...' Riya said.

'Maya, we know you were always close to Naina, but this is Riya's birthday weekend, and we are all meeting after such a long time. Do you think we could keep the weekend drama-free? Especially when Naina gets here. The truth is, ten years have passed, and we are not the same people we used to be,' Sam added.

I was a little hurt by Sam's tone. But then I looked at Riya and thought about the effort she had put into arranging this weekend and decided it was best if I remained quiet. Sam did have a point.

I tried to lighten the mood. 'Riya, I really don't want to be rude. I love sushi and the works, but I am in India and what I would really love to eat is some aloo ka paratha with the hottest pickle you have, and if you insist, fine, I'll have that glass of lassi, too.'

'I am so glad you said that. I hate sushi. I was only acting posh. Let me call Devi. She makes the most delectable parathas. And about the lassi, how about we spike it?' Riya said.

There was a sudden crackling sound in the room, followed by the wail of a baby. A baby? Was I hearing things? I looked around and noticed Riya had a baby monitor beside her. It was one of the latest models with a video feed and the camera was trained on a bassinet.

'Oops! The baby probably needs feeding,' Riya said.

'Wait a minute. You never told me you had a baby!'

'Well, if you had been in touch with me, I would have told you,' she replied coolly.

I ignored her tone. 'That's great news. I knew how much you always wanted a child.'

At that, Riya seemed to thaw a bit. 'I made it happen after a lot of blood, sweat and tears. Now if you will excuse me, please…'

'Did you know she had a baby?' I asked Sam after Riya had left the room.

'I only found out when I arrived,' Sam said.

Sam looked around and pulled her chair closer to mine and spoke in a whisper.

'Apparently the baby is only a couple of months old and has a respiratory issue, which is why Riya is very hush-hush about it. So, I suggest we don't bring up the baby ourselves and only talk about it if she does,' Sam said.

I nodded. This was turning out to be a very strange meeting. The dos and don'ts of talking to Riya were starting to annoy me. I prided myself on being open and transparent. But I understood Riya being a little touchy about the baby. We all knew how desperately she had wanted to become a mother, and I was glad it had finally worked out for her. But I was slowly learning there was so much I didn't know about my closest friends.

5

Riya rejoined us a couple of minutes later.

'Sorry guys, Bella needed a diaper change, so I took care of that and fixed her a bottle of milk. Now she's gone back to sleep,' Riya said.

'How is motherhood treating you, Riya?' Sam asked.

'It's the most rewarding experience of my life. It's like I waited my whole life to be a mother, and God finally blessed Yug and me. We couldn't be happier,' Riya said.

I almost felt like Sam had been overreacting. Riya seemed perfectly calm and did not appear high-strung about it at all.

Just then, Yug entered, surprising us all.

'Hello ladies, hope you aren't up to any mischief!' he teased.

'Hey, Yug. So good to see you,' I said, getting up to give him a quick hug.

I noticed he was in great shape, considering he was in his mid-forties. When we had first met him, he had been at Columbia University, pursuing an executive MBA. To our young selves, Yug was the epitome of sophistication and class. I suspected he might have had a hair transplant as I remembered him to have been balding when I last saw him, five years ago.

'Won't you join us for a bite? Devi is whipping up some parathas for us,' Sam said.

'I'd love to, but the wifey here has given me express instructions that this is to be a girls-only weekend. I am going over to a friend's place,' Yug said.

'Are you leaving right away? Please stay.' Riya pleaded.

'Sorry, I can't stay,' Yug responded curtly.

'Did you say bye to Bella?' Riya asked.

'Whatever for?' Yug sounded dismissive.

He saw the look of surprise on our faces and immediately corrected himself.

'I mean, of course, I have. Bella is an infant. It doesn't really make much of a difference to her. As long as somebody feeds her and changes her diaper, she's fine. Anyway, I better run.'

'Yug, can't you at least stay for a drink? It would mean so much to the girls.' Riya seemed to be begging.

'Well, okay,' Yug finally relented. 'I see you ladies are having champagne, but I'll need something stiffer.' He walked up to the bar and poured himself a large whisky. He took a couple of swigs of the single malt and quickly refilled his glass. I looked at Riya with concern. She seemed a little embarrassed by the entire interaction but stayed mum.

'So Maya, I heard you have become this bigshot attorney in New York,' Yug said.

'I don't know about bigshot, but yes, I specialise in immigration law and it's going well,' I said.

'Stop being so modest. I heard through the grapevine that you made it to partner. The youngest ever at your firm, I might add,' interjected Sam.

'Can we please talk about something else? This conversation is embarrassing me,' I said.

'So what have you girls planned for the weekend? Hope my wife is spoiling you good and proper,' Yug said.

'Yes, Parry and I do have some tricks up our sleeves,' Riya said.

'Parry! Now he's quite a character. Have you met him? Or is he hiding somewhere and will slither out once I've left, as usual?' Yug sounded bitter.

I noticed that the moment Riya had mentioned Parry's name, Yug's expression had changed. Who was Parry, anyway? And why did Yug dislike him so much? I decided to ask Riya about it later. I heard Yug's phone ringing. He answered it and asked the person on the line to hold on.

'So ladies, I need to be on my way. It was great seeing you all. Hopefully, when I am back, we will get to spend some time together,' Yug said and, with that, left without waiting for our response.

The exact moment that Yug left, Sam and I exchanged a knowing look. Both of us had sensed the tension between the couple. I had started feeling a little chilly, so I excused myself to go to my room and wear a sweater. On my way, I saw the driver in the corridor, carrying Yug's overnight bag in one hand.

6

I noticed that while Yug was with us, Riya had become noticeably quiet and withdrawn. Once he left, she spoke up before Sam or I could say anything.

'A baby really tests a marriage. We weren't always this way, but after Bella's arrival, things have seriously gone downhill. Yug feels I don't give him as much time any more, but I am just so exhausted all the time. Having a baby at forty is not easy. I have several postpartum issues. I wanted to breastfeed Bella, but mine was in short supply, so we had to resort to donated breast milk. Plus, my body is not what it used to be. I just feel insufficient, like I'm not good enough. It's just so hard,' Riya said tearily.

'My God, Riya, you are gorgeous. I think we women are way too hard on ourselves. It's only been a few months since you had Bella. Cut yourself some slack,' I said.

'If it helps, it was the same with Zayn and I when we had our girls. But it gets better. Trust me, just give it time,' Sam reassured her.

'Depends on what you consider to be better—do we just leave each other and get divorced? Because sometimes I think that's where we are headed. Yug's indifference towards Bella is hurtful, and frankly, we've waited so long to have a baby. Now that we have succeeded, it's like the common goal that was, in a way, holding us together no longer exists. We have drifted apart and barely seem to have anything in common.'

'It will change. Mark my words. Just be patient. I know it's easier said than done, but my love, you just need to hang in there.' Sam said sympathetically.

I changed the topic, seeing Riya get closer and closer to tears, 'Oh, come on, girls. There is so much to celebrate this weekend. Tell us more about your daughter, Riya, and more importantly, when can we see her?'

'Easy, my friend. You will get to meet Baby Bella very soon. She's sleeping right now. Want to take a quick peek?' Riya said.

'I'd love that,' I said. I followed Riya while Sam remained in the living room, replying to an urgent email. She had already met Bella earlier.

We walked down the hallway towards where my room was. I noticed Bella was in the room right next to mine. I made a mental note not to be too loud or take late-night work calls so I don't wake her. I noticed Riya take her shoes off before entering Bella's room, and I followed suit. 'Bella has the worst allergies, and with the pollution here, it only gets worse. My poor baby is only six months old and needs all the help in the world to breathe,' she explained.

I noticed Riya's eyes tear up when she talked about Bella. Right outside the room was a table with masks and sanitisers. We both wore a mask each and sanitised our hands. I guess with Bella's frail health, Riya was not taking any chances at all.

'I am sorry to hear that,' I said. It made sense now why Riya had behaved testily with Yug before.

We stepped into the room, onto a plush pink carpet. The walls were covered with a pink wallpaper with bunny rabbits on it. I noticed a hi-tech air purifier in one corner. Right in the centre of the room was a braided rattan bassinet. At the other end of the room, I noticed a huge open closet, filled with dresses for baby girls. There were toys in a transparent chest. A changing table and diaper pail stood at the other end of the room. The room looked like it was straight out of a home decor magazine. There was a five-foot teddy bear in one corner. Before we could walk over to Bella, there was a gentle knock on the door and Riya leapt up in fright. She signalled for me to leave the room with her. I understood, as Bella was sleeping and I knew parents do everything in their power not to wake the baby, choosing to enjoy the rare few minutes of peace and quiet.

We stepped outside the room.

'Devi, what the hell are you doing here?! I have told you a million times not to disturb me when I am with my Bella,' Riya screamed.

'Madamji, it was time for your medication,' Devi whispered and extended a cup of water and a handful of colourful pills towards Riya.

'Did you prepare the dose or Parry?'

'Parry Sir did before he went out.'

Riya gulped down the meds and we went back to the living room and refilled our glasses with champagne. Who was Parry? And why was everybody talking about him?

7

We rejoined Sam in the living room. She had sent off her emails and was now showing us photos of her girls.

'Sam, the girls are so cute. How old are they?' I asked.

'Kinza is four years old and Sana is two,' Sam said with a look of pride.

'I think they both look like you. That's why they are so gorgeous,' Riya said.

'I love that you make them wear the same outfits.'

'It's easier that way or else they will fight,' Sam said.

'That's hilarious.'

'Girls, I just need to make a few calls, so if you could please excuse me,' Riya said.

After Riya's departure, Sam and I were finally free to have a much-needed conversation. For a couple of minutes, there was silence. The reason behind our mutual awkwardness had to do with our graduation. Naina had closed up around us the night before, and I thought her odd behaviour had to do with the fact that our college life was coming to an end. We all had day-to-day struggles and stress, but despite that, there was a carefreeness when we got together that we would never feel again after we graduated. The following morning, Sam and I woke up early to get our hair done. We were splurging, but we wanted to look our best at our graduation ceremony. We found a trainee hairstylist from Vidal Sassoon who agreed to do our hair for very cheap.

We noticed Naina was nowhere to be found and that she had taken her overnight bag with her. Assuming she'd join us at the hairstylist, we went on with our plans, but she never showed up. Only she and I had been at law school together. Sam was doing a different course, and we were lucky that our graduation ceremonies were being held on the same day. We attended without Naina, and after the ceremony, Yug offered to take us out for a celebratory dinner at Ai Fiori at the Langham Hotel. Sam had decided to skip and instead spend time with her Pakistani-American boyfriend, Zayn. The next morning, when she had returned to the apartment, she had excitedly announced that Zayn had popped the question, the previous night, and she was going to City Hall so they could get married. She needed a witness and had asked me, but I had felt like she was rushing into it and declined. So instead, Riya had agreed to be a witness, and I had got into a row with Sam because I thought her marrying Zayn was a big mistake and that she would come to regret her decision later, as he clearly spelled trouble. And I couldn't just stand and watch Sam blowing up her life in flames. She went ahead and married him anyway. That weekend changed our lives forever.

Although Sam and I had kept in touch and met a few times over the years, there had always been a distance between us; my residual disapproval at her hasty marriage.

'All good?' I asked.

'I guess so. How have you been, Maya? It's been a while since I've heard from you. What happened?' Sam asked.

'Life happened.'

'It had something to do with Zayn, right? Don't say I told you so, but you were right about him. Our relationship was doomed from the start. But what was I to do? I was besotted and blinded. No amount of reasoning with me would have worked.' Sam's tone was regretful.

'The last thing I want to do, Sam, is to put salt on your wounds. I am here for you no matter what happened with Zayn.'

'It's like graduation happened and our group just scattered. Of all people, it's Riya who has brought us all together again—the one who, ironically, never even attended school with us.'

'I know. The important thing to remember is that we're not getting any younger, and it is high time for us to come together. Which is why I got us bottles of our favourite vodka; shots are in order later this evening,' I said.

'Belvedere? No way, Maya. It's been ages since I had that.' Riya said, walking back into the room.

'Let me go fetch the bottle from the refrigerator,' I said. I brought the bottle and then walked over to the bar to pull out some shot glasses. I generously poured the vodka into them.

'Gosh, how did we drink this stuff straight up? It's lethal!' Riya said.

'I know, right?' Sam said.

The alcohol soon kicked in, and I started to feel all light and floaty. Very soon, I knew I would crave a cigarette. For a moment, I regretted not buying a pack at the airport.

My tongue was loosened by the vodka, and I asked my burning question: 'Sam, what's with the burqa? It's very fetching.'

'This is how I roll now, my friend.' Sam winked. 'Jokes apart, though, it was more to show respect to Zayn and his family. Being an Indian Muslim, I was not pious enough for them and had to prove my faith and allegiance to Islam by wearing a burqa. And frankly, it looks worse than it actually is—I can be fat or skinny; it's all hidden. I don't need to spend hours trying to figure out what I want to wear. I have only black and blue burqas to pick from. I do believe we tend to spend so much time on the irrelevant stuff. The time that would have been spent fretting over clothes, I now spend with my girls instead,' Sam said.

'That's awesome. I did, however, once read that in more conservative countries, women wear the most outlandish, expensive designer-label wear under their abayas. And when they congregate, they remove their abayas and become unrecognisable.'

'It's so funny you say that. During Eid or the odd wedding or dinner party, Zayn constantly pesters me to wear my Dior dress with four-inch high heels. But I just couldn't be bothered. Under the abaya, nobody really cares.'

It was almost like Sam had resigned herself to her fate. Of all of us, Sam was always the most fashion-conscious. We often visited Goodwill and thrift stores just so we could rummage through the clothes, and then Sam would style some pieces in the most fashionable way possible. And now, so many years later, fashion is the last thing on Sam's mind. That's how much we all have changed.

Further emboldened by the shots, I asked another question that was on my mind. 'Riya, I keep hearing this Parry's name. Who is he?'

Riya burst out laughing. 'You will get to meet him tomorrow. He's hard to miss. Right now, he's busy running around like a headless chicken making arrangements for my dinner party tomorrow. The storm has completely thrown him off.'

We managed to down a few more shots before we all started yawning. There was a big day ahead of us—Naina was finally going to arrive. We said our goodnights and retired to our rooms. I went to the bathroom, brushed my teeth and washed my face. I pulled out my anti-ageing cream from Kiehl's and applied it all over my face. I was on the wrong side of thirty-five and needed all the help I could get to preserve my youthful appearance. I then changed into my pyjamas and pulled out my Kindle, looking around in vain for a power outlet to charge my phone. Finally, I located one, wedged between the TV cabinet and the wall. I then noticed I had an even bigger problem—I was not carrying my US–India adapter. I had only 20 per cent battery left on my phone, and I did not want to bother Riya this late at night. I stepped outside to see if anybody was around to help me. I noticed the door to Bella's bedroom was open. I peeked inside and leapt up in fright when I saw someone wearing something like a hazmat suit.

I peered closely and exclaimed, 'Devi?! What in God's name are you wearing?'

'I am cleaning Bella Baby's room. All precautions have to be taken because of her condition,' Devi said.

I nodded. I understood that Bella was an infant and had health issues, but a get-up like this seemed a little excessive.

'Can you tell me where I can find an adapter or a charger for my phone?'

'Sure. Follow me, Madamji,' Devi said.

I followed Devi back into my room, and she opened the drawer below the TV cabinet to hand me a charger before disappearing into the night in her creepy outfit.

8

I turned off the light and the room got very dark. I always had trouble sleeping in new places, and the fancy automatic blackout blinds that Riya had put up did not help. I turned on the light in the bathroom and left the door slightly ajar, unable to find another night light. As soon as I lay down, I started to feel my eyes get heavier.

Suddenly, I woke up with a jolt. I looked at the clock and it was 4 a.m. I had been asleep for two hours. *What was that noise?* I looked towards the door; I could hear footsteps outside. I was too groggy and sleep-deprived; could I be imagining things? I had taken off my contact lenses, so I reached for my glasses. Softly making my way to the door, I could no longer hear any footsteps, just the click of the front door shutting. I peered through the peephole and could only make out the elevator door closing. I stayed there for a couple of minutes before returning to my room. I knew I wasn't going to go back to sleep immediately.

Earlier in the evening, I had spotted a pack of cigarettes in the living room credenza. Apparently, Yug was an occasional smoker. I grabbed the pack and made my way to Riya's living room balcony. It was a moonless night and there was a light breeze. The construction workers had long gone, and there wasn't a soul to be seen, unlike New York, where even at 3 a.m., the city was bustling with activity. I finished my cigarette and was about to head back inside when I heard a loud crashing sound. I looked down from the balcony and saw a figure run out of the apartment building as if they were being chased by demons. Before I could react, the person disappeared into the darkness. It made me uneasy, and I wanted to quickly return to the safety of my room and lock the door.

I quickly left the balcony, closing the door softly so as not to wake anybody. The hallway was empty. I tiptoed back into my room and heaved a huge sigh of relief. I lay down and heard a noise again. My room shared a wall with Bella's. Had the sound come from her room? Maybe she had woken up. Or perhaps it was coming from outside my window. I knew I would not be able to sleep until I had located the source of the noise. I decided to investigate and pressed the button to draw the automatic shades. A masked figure stood outside. I sprang back in fear and scrambled out of the room when I crashed into someone and screamed.

'Maya, are you okay?' Sam said.

'Oh sorry. Thank God it's you, Sam. Can you follow me to my room? There is someone outside,' I said.

I could tell from the uncertain expression on Sam's face that she thought I was crazy. She followed me back to my room. We looked around and there was nobody there. I had been so certain but now I felt silly, like I'd overreacted.

'Look, there's no one here,' Sam consoled me. 'Besides, they would have had to jump from the balcony attached to Bella's room and hang from the ledge just to scare you.'

Sam's explanation made sense, but I was unable to shake off the feeling that something didn't add up. 'I'm sorry, Sam. I thought I saw a masked figure outside my room. Maybe I was imagining it. All that alcohol was probably not the best idea with my jet lag. How come you are up?'

'Went to offer namaz on the roof deck. It's quite beautiful up there. You should check it out. Anyway, I'll try to get some sleep now. We have a long day ahead,' Sam said.

I could tell Sam was lying because she was not carrying a prayer mat with her. Could she have been woken up by the same sound as me?

I knew trying to sleep would be pointless at this stage. I had long suffered from anxiety, and when I lay down, I started getting palpitations. I felt a tightening in my chest. I resisted the urge to Google my symptoms, so I logged into my email instead and started responding to work emails. So much for being on holiday! I was almost beginning to feel like one of those sad workaholics who had no life outside of their work.

But I couldn't remain distracted for long. I was still a little uncomfortable about my interaction with Sam a couple of minutes ago. I felt like I had overreacted, and since we had only recently reconnected, I did not want her to think I had lost my mind. I decided to go speak to her. I knocked on her door, and there was no response, but the door had been left slightly ajar. I peeked inside and noticed that Sam's bathroom light was on. Then I heard a loud gasp. I wasn't sure if I should go and check if she was okay, but then I could tell from the movement in the bathroom that she was on her way out. Sure enough, she stepped out of the toilet, wearing black pyjamas with a beige camisole. I noticed her arms were covered in scars. I also noticed a deeper cut, a straight red line on her left arm. It looked like a fresh wound, and, unless I was mistaken, Sam was likely self-harming again.

'Could you excuse me for a minute?' Sam looked embarrassed at being caught off-guard.

I waited for her. She returned a couple of minutes later, wearing her burqa. It was clear her attire was a great cover-up for her scars.

'Sam, why?' I was unable to keep the fear and concern out of my voice.

'What do you mean?'

'You know what I am referring to.'

'Life is not easy, Maya.'

'I know, but this is not good for you.'

'Just like drinking like a fish isn't good for you,' she countered.

I ignored her hurtful jibe for the moment and shifted the focus back to her. This was not about me.

'Can't you get help?'

'I can't. I don't know how to say this, but Zayn uses our daughters as pawns in our fights, and this is the only way I feel safe releasing my pent-up anxiety. Anything else I do could potentially be used against me in the battle for my children's custody. I could lose them.'

'Have things progressed that far? Are you that close to getting divorced?'

'I am not. I wish Zayn had cheated or worse. But he's just a layabout and we have grown apart. He doesn't want to work, and the financial stress of providing for the family is getting to me. I run a non-profit, not a million-dollar company. We are eating through our petty savings, and it's not long before we land on the street. Only I know the enormous stress I am going through. Each day is agonising for me. It's only my girls that keep me going. I can't risk something happening to me and them being raised by Zayn. I never envisioned my life would turn out this way.'

'How long have you been feeling like this?' I realised that Sam had kept her emotions bottled up fairly well. By my earlier interactions, I would never have been able to guess the hardships she was going through.

'Since the time I got married. I was just never good enough, and every friend, family member and acquaintance of Zayn's made it a point to rub that in. What they didn't realise was that

Zayn and I had struggles of our own—we'd discovered we had fundamental compatibility issues which surfaced once we got married and started living together.'

'I hope you know that's not true at all—no one has the right to make you feel small,' I jumped to my friend's defence.

'Initially, I knew it wasn't true, but after a while, you can't help but start believing those lies,' Sam said, her eyes welling up with tears.

'I wish I could say or do something to change your mind because the person I see before me, the person I know, is strong and capable.'

'Will you please stay? Let's watch some silly YouTube videos and not sleep.'

'Absolutely! But only after we raid Riya's fridge.'

Like everything in Riya's house, the contents of the fridge were labelled and arranged by colour. We pulled out a jar of jalapeño hummus and celery sticks. I opened the freezer to get some ice cream and saw it was full of packets of breast milk.

I found a tub of Ben & Jerry's cookies and cream ice cream, and we both went back to my room to watch old episodes of *The Bachelor*. Only twenty minutes had passed before Sam started nodding off and had to return to her room to get a few hours of sleep.

I still couldn't sleep and considered asking Devi to make me some turmeric milk to soothe my frayed nerves. But I looked around and couldn't find her anywhere. I noticed there was a narrow corridor leading to a room outside the kitchen, which I guessed was Devi's. I walked over and knocked gently on the open door. I called out to Devi but got no response. I noticed a piece of paper on the nightstand—a one-way bus ticket to some place called Shivpuri. Was Devi leaving?

9

I woke up in the morning feeling quite refreshed, despite having barely got any sleep.

I went into the bathroom and freshened up. When I returned to my room and was about to change, I heard a gentle knock on the door. I opened the door, and Devi was standing outside, holding a steaming cup of coffee. I had almost forgotten about the perks of living in India. I gratefully took the cup from her and closed the door. Mornings always made me feel upbeat, and I decided to push all the negative thoughts out of my head and enjoy the weekend with my girlfriends. Sam and I had made up, and now the only one I'd left on bad terms with was Naina, whom I would get to see later in the day. I had my coffee and checked my email—everything seemed to be in control, which was a relief. I looked at my watch, it was 7 a.m. I was sure nobody else would be up, so I planned a little surprise for them. I was not a fantastic cook, but the one thing I knew how to make well was French toast bread pudding, which Sam and Naina had taught me ages ago.

Back in uni, I was dating an Indian-American guy called Arjun. Even today, when I think about it, I find it hard to define what our relationship really was. We were just together. Around Thanksgiving, he invited me to spend the holiday with his family. Under normal circumstances, getting invited to a Thanksgiving dinner meant pretty much introducing 'the one' to your family. Except, our situation was different. We knew it wasn't going to last. But I was still flattered and touched that he had invited me. I offered to bring along some frozen cornbread from Trader Joe's, to which Arjun flatly told me that his mom loved to cook everything from scratch. I went back to our apartment stressed out, not knowing what to take along. Sam and Naina came up with the perfect brunch recipe and after a couple of attempts, I was pretty sure I could whip up something good. Riya loaned me a scarlet cashmere turtleneck to wear to the Thanksgiving dinner. The night of the dinner was uneventful, and I sensed Arjun's mother was a tough cookie. I made blunder after blunder in the kitchen, embarrassing myself, but was surprised to see how she dealt with it all so kindly, even though she ended up making the bread pudding pretty much by herself. But if there was one thing I wasn't, it was a quitter. I practised nonstop after that incident until I had perfected the bread pudding recipe. Arjun and I eventually decided to go our separate ways, but the bread pudding was here to stay.

I entered Riya's kitchen and couldn't help but admire how immaculate and up-to-date it was. A true chef's kitchen. I went to the refrigerator and pulled out some eggs, milk and cream. Riya had white bread but not challah bread. I decided to use an extra egg and hoped it would work. I started looking around for a pot and a whisk until I saw someone enter the kitchen. It was Devi. She immediately rushed towards me and told me to go rest and that she would prepare breakfast. I told her I wanted to make a special dish. She looked perplexed that a house guest wanted to work in the kitchen. Finally, she relented, and I started whisking the eggs, cream and sugar together with a pinch of salt, vanilla essence and lemon and orange zests in a big pot. I noticed Devi lurking in the background. She was staring at me, but not inquisitively, just wearing a blank look. I tried to ignore her stare until, from the corner of my eye, I saw her wipe her eyes. I paused and walked over to her.

'Devi, are you all right?'

'Yes, Madamji,' Devi said wiping away her tears. I placed my hands on her shoulders.

'Is something bothering you? You can talk to me, and I promise it will stay between us.'

'I miss my daughters, Madamji. I have three daughters back in my village, and I haven't seen them in a long time. I miss them,' Devi said, crying and shaking uncontrollably.

'I know what you mean. I live in a big city like you, Devi, away from my family. And sometimes, I miss them terribly, too, but I also know that I need to make a living.'

Devi nodded. I understood—for all my professional accomplishments, there was still an indescribable loneliness in my life, which I knew Devi felt, too. I wanted to ask her about the bus ticket I had found in her room but decided not to, considering she was so upset. But it was all starting to make sense now.

'Devi, were you, by any chance, in Bella's room last night?'

'Bella Baby's room?'

'Yes, must have been around midnight, I think?'

'No, Madamji. I was sleeping.'

If the person outside my room wasn't Devi, then who was it?

'Madamji, is there anything else I can do for you? It's time for me to wake up Riya Madamji,' Devi said, wiping away more tears. She was now holding a tray with various shots—apple cider vinegar, wheatgrass and something black, that was probably for anti-ageing or something.

'Go ahead, I am almost done here.' I assembled my bread pudding and cranked up the oven. Once it was pre-heated, I popped the pudding in. I then started preparing the strawberry compote. I added some orange zest, lemon zest and powdered sugar and stirred it all in gently. Once that was ready, I waited for the bread pudding to rise and get a beautiful golden crust. When I pulled it out, I was glad to see that the custard had set beautifully. No brunch was complete without mimosas, so I opened the refrigerator and pulled out a bottle of Prosecco. There was also a container of fresh orange juice. Brunch was ready.

I was about to leave the kitchen and head back to my room when I noticed that in one corner, sitting on top of kitchen towels, were a pair of sparkly gold ballet flats that I had seen Devi wearing the previous day. Upon closer inspection, I noticed the soles were covered in fresh mud and a few crushed bougainvillaea flowers from the only flowering plant around this otherwise desolate building. I felt pretty sure that the person I had seen running away scared had been Devi. What had she been so afraid of? Why had she lied to me that she had been sleeping when she had clearly not? What was Devi so desperate to hide? Whatever the reason, was it enough to have made her want to run away from Riya's house? I was jet-lagged and sleep-deprived myself, so could I just be reading too much into everything? I shrugged off the feeling of uneasiness and looked at the bread pudding I'd made with pride, before deciding to get on with my day.

I pulled out a pair of blue jeans and a black T-shirt and slipped on my navy blue Toms. I went back to the living room to look for Riya and Sam. I noticed there was nobody around. I saw Devi dusting the windows. I immediately thought of the conversation I had had with her in the morning. I had been practising law for a while now, so I could read people very well. If my hunch was right, there was something up with

Devi and she seemed scared, very scared. Like me, quitting was not really an option for her, either. It was natural for her to miss her daughters, but what I had witnessed in the kitchen seemed more than a mere bout of homesickness—there was fear in her eyes. I needed to have a conversation with her at some point. Even though it was really none of my business, I couldn't just ignore a person in distress, especially if they were crying this loudly for help.

'Devi, do you know where the other madams are? Are they awake?' I asked.

'They are upstairs, on the roof deck, waiting for you,' Devi said.

'Great, do you think you could help me take the breakfast up to them?'

Devi nodded. I was glad she was looking a lot more composed now. But I made a mental note anyway to mention her odd behaviour to Riya, so she could have a word with her. Maybe Devi would be more comfortable talking to her than me, an absolute stranger.

I thanked her and we made our way to the kitchen. We assembled everything on a tray and went to the roof deck. I saw Riya and Sam having tea. They waved towards me.

'Maya, isn't it gorgeous up here?' Riya asked. We were all sitting under an awning as it had started to rain a lot harder, and I could see that it was only going to get worse as the day progressed.

'It is lovely,' I said. With the rain crashing, we felt completely cut off from the world. To think only a few kilometres from here, the rest of Gurugram was bustling with activity.

'Really cool, right? You know, when this project was announced, I pestered Yug that we *had* to come live here. They plan to make this a super-private, all-amenities-included residential complex,' Riya said. 'Though there's still some way to go.'

'Did they also have you undergo some sort of a vetting process before you moved in?' I asked jokingly, thinking back to the crazy interview I had had with a cooperative society board once, only to then be rejected because I had a pet cat and the building only allowed service dogs.

'They did, actually. Like I said, it's super-exclusive. You have to have a certain profile, educational background, and more importantly, net worth, to own a place here,' she said proudly.

Sam started laughing.

'Okay fine, ladies, I get the joke. They only care about your net worth. But now I've got cosy with the management, and we are trying to get only those families in that are somewhat like-minded.'

'So, are there any other residents yet?' Sam asked.

'Well, there is a doctor who recently moved in, and I think another lady, who is single and maybe in her seventies. She lives on her own and doesn't like to interact much with people. But they expect full occupancy by spring. That's actually another reason why Yug is so miserable. He was against us leaving the house he grew up in. He feels like this part of the city is too in the back of the beyond.'

'It *is* a little lonely and secluded out here,' I said with a shudder. I couldn't quite put my finger on it, but moving into an apartment complex that was still under construction did seem a little crazy. Especially since Riya and Yug's financial status permitted them to move into a better service apartment to wait out in the interim.

'Yes, but I needed a fresh start for our new family. Once Bella came into our lives, I decided I had played by the rules for too long. The house we lived in felt suffocating—the decor hadn't been changed in fifty years, and even though it was located in a much sought-after neighbourhood, it never felt like my own. But this is all mine,' Riya said, looking around proudly.

I noticed some cookies on the tea table and grabbed one.

'Maya, I can't believe you made your French toast bread pudding!' exclaimed Sam.

'There goes my diet. You know I can't resist your bread pudding, Maya,' said Riya.

'Guys, considering it's the only thing I know how to make, I'd say enjoy it while it lasts,' I passed around plates and forks to Riya and Sam. I served them large slices and poured compote over them, despite their protests.

'Are you still in touch with that bread pudding guy?' Riya asked.

'You mean Arjun? Nope. But I did do some snooping around, and I think he's now the proud daddy of three-year-old twin girls.'

'I guess all's well that ends well. Right now, I can't focus on anything but this delectable bread pudding,' she answered.

'While you ladies dig in, I have another surprise for you. Since this promises to be a crazy weekend, we are drippin',' Riya said, laughing.

'Drippin'?' I asked.

'Yes, my lovely ladies. Drippin'.' I heard a male voice. I turned around and saw a man walking up to us. He was around five feet ten and had an athletic build; his hair fell to his shoulders, and he looked no older than twenty-three. He reminded me of Salman Khan in *Maine Pyar Kiya*. He was wearing skinny black ripped jeans and a white shirt with the buttons opened halfway, black aviator sunglasses and Chuck Taylors.

'Maya and Sam, meet Parry. My man Friday, confidant, nanny, everything rolled into one,' Riya explained, her face lighting up at the sight of him.

'Hello, ladies. Let's just say I wear many hats. I have heard so much about you both, and it's really nice to finally meet you in person,' Parry said, extending his hand.

'Well, Parry here distracted us, but I was going to explain what drippin' is. An intravenous line will be hooked up to our arms to give us hydration and nutrition which will replenish all our bodies' essential nutrients. Then we'll be super fit and fabulous for the night ahead,' Riya said.

'Are you sure about this?' Sam asked, uncomfortable.

'Of course. It's super safe. Just consider it a concentrated shot of vitamin C and boom, all done,' Parry said.

'Well, if you insist,' Sam said.

'I have set it up for you ladies downstairs, so please make your way there whenever you are ready,' Parry said and then took our leave.

Riya could see the questioning look on Sam and my face.

'Isn't he a delight?' Riya said.

'Well, what's the deal here?' I asked.

'I needed someone to help me out with the day-to-day running of the house. Especially someone educated. So I posted an advertisement and Parry applied. I was surprised such a well-qualified guy would want to work as a glorified butler. But it looked like he had bigger plans. He wants to pursue fashion and for that, he needed to live in a big city, but he comes from a humble background. He went to English-medium schools, but the town he lived in did not promise him much of a future in fashion. So he signed up for a part-time fashion designing course. He gets a small stipend from us, along with free food and a place to stay, so it has all worked out really well for him and for us, too.'

Well, that explained Parry. For the moment, at least. I could finally rest easy.

'Girls, I would have loved to take you out and show you around some of my favourite spots in Delhi. But the weather forecast does not look good, and I would hate for us to get stranded. I guess we are marooned in my beautiful apartment for the entire weekend,' Riya said.

'No worries, Riya. The idea is to spend time together. Besides, Maya, aren't you flying out in two days?' Sam asked.

'I am, unfortunately. I have a court appearance to go to, next week, or else I would have definitely stayed longer,' I said.

'What a pity. Wish you could have extended your stay. But anyway, the important thing is that you made it,' Riya said.

'Any idea what Naina's plan is?' I asked.

'Well, I know for a fact that she's coming tonight,' Riya said.

'How long has she been in Delhi?' Sam asked.

'Frankly, I don't have any details. I reached out to Naina, as I have multiple times in the last couple of years, on her old uni email. As always, I was not expecting her to reply. But to my utter surprise and delight, she actually responded this time around. She always seemed very rushed and curt in her responses. I'm guessing it's because she wants to catch up with us in person,' Riya said.

'I am just glad she's coming,' I said.

'That reminds me, I need to go check on Bella and a few other things before the dinner tonight,' Riya said, getting up.

'When are we meeting the little love bug again?' I asked.

'Hopefully soon. This pollution is not good for her. She needs to be in a clean environment, and with all these viruses going around, it's really stressful. So, we have to sort of quarantine her.'

'Totally get that. We have a lifetime to get to know her and spend time with her, after all. Can't believe I am an aunt to three lovely young ladies,' I said.

Riya got up and left. Sam and I were lying on the lounge chairs. I was about to say something when I noticed she had dozed off. The conversation about marriage and babies got me thinking if I would ever have that in my life. I thought of Naina and how we both were sailing in the same boat—or so I assumed. I had no idea what she was up to. Who knew? Maybe she was a mother of four, living on some remote island with no internet. That would explain why she hadn't kept in touch. I quietly got up and left so as not to disturb Sam.

After the drippin', I spent the rest of the afternoon watching old episodes of *The Bachelor* on my laptop mindlessly. I looked at my watch and realised that in an hour, we were to gather for dinner. I still had no idea what time Naina was coming. I turned on my laptop, and there was still no response to my email. I then Googled Naina Kumari, and a few irrelevant results showed up. I refined my search and looked for 'Naina Kumari NYU'. Nothing. I noticed Naina had no Instagram page, LinkedIn, Facebook or Twitter. I closed my laptop in frustration. I got up and went to the bathroom to freshen up. I opened the bathroom window, looked outside, and spotted some sort of a delivery vehicle that had somehow made its way here despite the terrible weather. I saw Parry unloading boxes and Riya standing nearby, watching and mouthing some sort of instructions to him. He was dressed from head to toe in fashionable raingear, ready to take on any storm. I saw Devi scowling in a corner, taking some of the bags from Parry and leaving to bring them upstairs. Parry and Riya disappeared into the building as well, soon after, and I could tell they were coming back upstairs. I saw the delivery truck backing out and turning onto the uneven road. I also noticed a young man standing in a corner with a box in his hands. He looked up at the building before slowly making his way inside.

I turned to look at myself in the mirror. For some reason, I was unable to brush off the jitteriness I was feeling. Perhaps I was still exhausted. Usually, going on a run would help me clear my head; I could only look outside in dismay. I went over to my suitcase and pulled out a pair of Lululemon tights with a matching T-shirt. Even though I was looking for a high-intensity workout, I would have to settle for yoga-style stretches for the time being. I stepped outside my room and saw Parry.

'Hey, Parry.'

'Yes?'

'Do you, by any chance, have a yoga mat lying around somewhere?'

'Oh yes, I do.'

Parry led me to a room at the back. I noticed a walking desk—essentially a desk with a treadmill belt built into it for people who wanted to work out even while they worked. I spotted the huge iMac sitting on the desk. Parry saw me taking it all in.

'Well, this is Yug's workstation and he is a fitness fanatic. So even while he is taking calls or sending out emails, he stays on the move.'

'Oh cool!'

'Want to give it a shot? I think there is a speed limit on it, but you could definitely use it for a light jog.'

'I'd love to. I was craving a run, but thanks to the weather, I couldn't go. Can you give me a couple of minutes to go get my sneakers?'

'Maya, I have a bunch of chores I need to take care of; do you think I could teach you how this machine works and then take my leave?'

Parry explained the basic functions of the treadmill to me. When I returned from my room, I noticed that a white hand towel, an energy bar and a chilled bottle of evian had been placed in a corner of the desk for me.

I went back to the treadmill, stepped onto it and decided to avoid running, in case I damaged it in some way. I put in my AirPods and started listening to Tupac, walking briskly. A couple of seconds later, I noticed the movement had made Yug's screen come alive.

Surprisingly, it wasn't password-protected. I leaned in and noticed it had synced to his iPhone. There was a notification that his flight to London was leaving in forty-five minutes, and they were ready to board. I didn't recall anyone mentioning Yug was going to London and thought he was out having a boys' weekend somewhere close by. I soon realised I was privy to information I wasn't supposed to have. Last thing I wanted was for Riya to think I was intruding upon their life. I stepped off the treadmill, spotted a yoga mat in the corner, grabbed it and went back to my room to process what I had just learned about Yug.

10

I did a couple of stretches but my heart wasn't in it. I was still reeling from the information I had uncovered. I went to the bathroom, peeled off my sweaty clothes and stepped under the shower. As soon as the hot water hit my body, I let out a sigh of relief. My body was sore after the long flight, and the water felt really good. I could feel my tense muscles relaxing. A couple of minutes later, I stepped out and grabbed two fluffy towels. Wrapping one around my body and the other around my head before turning to open the door, I found it would not budge. I struggled with the handle a few times but to no avail. Closed spaces made me feel suffocated. I threw my body against the door, banged on it loudly, screamed for help, but nobody came. I tried the door handle again, and this time, it opened. I stepped out of the bathroom and frantically looked around. Everything looked the same. I tried out the bathroom door again—it opened and closed easily. Strange. I walked towards my suitcase and pulled out clean undergarments. Exhaustion and my mind seemed to be playing tricks on me. I looked at the clock and realised I had no time to stand around. I had to get dressed.

I pulled out a work dress that looked festive enough; I had bought it from Theory. I was just about to slip into it when I heard a gentle knock on the door.

'Yes?'

'Maya, it's me, Parry.'

I was slightly annoyed at the untimely interruption.

'Can you please wait? I am in the middle of something.'

'Take your time, honey.'

I hurriedly slipped on a T-shirt and shorts and opened the door. Parry was holding a bag in his hand. 'Riya's fortieth swag bag,' he said.

'Swag bag?'

'Go ahead, open it,' he said. The bag had 'Riya's 40th' written on it.

I took it inside my room and opened it. There was a black onesie with 'Riya's 40th' written across the back, a bejewelled eye mask, collagen mask, candy, two cans of rosé and fluffy slippers.

'I put all this together in twenty-four hours. Once I knew the storm was coming and you ladies would be having a slumber party here, I knew I had to come up with something extraordinary for Riya,' he said proudly.

'I am impressed, but aren't we too old to be having a … slumber party, as you call it?'

'Honey, you're never too old to do goofy stuff,' he said.

With that, he left the room, and I had to admit he did have a point.

I put on the outfit and looked at myself in the mirror. I did look goofy. I went to my suitcase and pulled out Riya's birthday gift. Even though she was a dear friend, I had been very confused about what to get her. I knew she had always liked luxury goods, so I got her a pair of custom champagne flutes from Baccarat to commemorate her fortieth birthday. They were fancy and expensive, and I was sure she would like them. As lovely as she was, she loved the finer things in life.

With Sam and Naina, it had always been easier. Sam loved cooking, especially Italian food. I had made a trip to the Eataly store and bought her a box of black truffle mushrooms. She often joked that in an earlier life, she had probably been a Nonna with eight grandkids, living in an old Italian village and cooking up a storm to feed her brood. Naina loved reading, and one of her all-time favourite books was *Jane Eyre*. I chanced upon an early edition on an auction site and promptly purchased it for her, even though I wasn't sure if she was coming.

I applied some light make-up and made my way to the living room. I placed the bags containing everyone's gifts in a corner. I was the first one to arrive. I noticed that candles had been lit all over the room, and there were vases holding long-stemmed white roses. It looked beautiful, and I felt a little foolish in the onesie. I noticed Sam walk in wearing the same onesie as me, except that she had a headscarf on. We both looked at each other and burst out laughing. There was champagne on a side table; we poured ourselves a glass each and waited for Naina to arrive and for Riya to join us. I could hear 'Gabriel's Oboe' playing in the background. The storm was raging—the rain was falling hard against the windowpane, and one could see lightning from time to time. The apartment felt warm and cosy. Riya entered in her typical style, wearing her onesie with high heels. But she was the birthday girl, so she was allowed to be a little over-the-top. Tagging along with her was Parry, wearing the same pyjama set as all of us. I guessed he was joining us, too.

'Ladies, this weekend is all about you and pampering yourself. I have another surprise for you,' Parry announced.

'Let me guess—strippers?' Riya said cheekily.

'Naughty, Riya,' Parry said.

As an employee, I felt like Parry crossed the line a lot with Riya, but for some reason, she didn't seem to mind it. It was almost like she was mesmerised by him, and he could do no wrong in her eyes.

'Well, I have arranged for some special spa treatments for you ladies,' Parry said.

'Have you, really? My goodness, that sounds like a fantastic idea! I could really do with some pampering. I don't know the last time I actually treated myself to a mani-pedi or even a massage,' Sam said.

'Now Sammy, I want you to put your feet up and relax,' Riya said putting her arm around Sam.

'Come on. Follow me,' Parry said.

We all followed Parry into a room lit by some more candles and burning incense sticks. In the background, we could hear German musician Karunesh's tracks playing. I noticed two massage tables had been set up, and there were two pedicurists.

'Do we wait for Naina?' I asked.

'I think we should start. God knows what time she is getting here. Besides, with the way the weather is, these ladies might have to cut short our treatments and leave, if necessary,' Riya said.

Riya decided on getting a massage, and Sam and I opted for pedicures. I selected the lavender spa pedicure, but as soon as the pedicurist started, the smell of lavender became nauseating. I noticed Devi standing outside the room, and this time, instead of lurking, she was staring directly at me. I knew she wanted to speak to me. Maybe it was Ravi from the front gate again; maybe Naina had sent word. With Sam and Riya busy with their own spa treatments, I knew this was my best chance to talk to Devi alone. I took the opportunity to let the pedicurist know I was having a headache and excused myself. I pulled my feet out of the tub of warm water and wiped them with a towel nearby.

I left the spa room and signalled Devi to join me in my bedroom.

'There you are, my dear. Was the pedicure no good? Not up to New York standards?' Parry asked.

'Well, it's more like I am sleep-deprived and suffering from a headache, so I thought I would get some Advil instead. Long evening ahead, you see.'

'Do you mind if I join you? There is something I need to talk to you about.'

'Can it wait?'

'Promise it won't take more than a couple of minutes. Pretty please?'

'Sure.' I was annoyed at Parry's intrusion, but I also knew him enough to understand that he was not going to let me be until he had had a word with me. I had seen how tenacious he got with Riya. I reached my room and pulled out two Advil from my handbag, swallowing them without any water, like a pro. I would have to wait for at least half an hour before they kicked in. And before that, I would have to endure Parry along with the horrible headache.

'Well, Maya, I am in love with someone,' he said dramatically.

'That's great.' *And irrelevant*, I thought secretly. Parry barely knew me, so making such a grand declaration before me made no sense.

'The only issue is John Jay, who I lovingly call JJ, does not live in India but in New York.' Parry paused dramatically to wait for my reaction.

'Okay?'

'I recently got my tourist visa, and as soon as I land in New York, JJ and I are planning on tying the knot at City Hall. After our marriage, I believe JJ can file for my green card since same-sex marriages are recognised in New York?'

'That is correct.'

'Well, I have heard that these cases can get really complicated. So I was hoping you could help me out, just so there are no unnecessary delays.'

'Sure. Let me grab my card. As soon as you land in New York, give me a call and let's see what we can do.'

'Another thing, Maya.'

'Yup?'

'Can you not mention any of this to Riya? Postpartum, she has gotten a little loopy in the head. She won't like the fact that I am leaving, especially since how things are going with Yug.'

'What about Yug?' I barely knew Parry and would have saved this conversation for Riya. But what I had learned about Yug going to London without telling Riya anything about it was a little perplexing.

'Oh my God, I am drinking too much and shooting my mouth off. Please forgive me. Anyway, I bet Riya is looking for me. I should get back to her.'

I stood for a couple of minutes not knowing what the purpose of this conversation was. Maybe moving thousands of miles for love was a bit intimidating for Parry. And what was that about Yug? I felt like it was a little bait Parry had thrown in to spark my interest. I was pretty sure he had no intention of telling me anything, even though he knew exactly what was going on between the couple. I would have to bide my time and check in with Riya as to what was really going on between Yug and her when the time was right.

I went back to the spa room and noticed the ladies packing up. Sam informed me that it had started raining heavily and they didn't want to get stranded, which made sense. An Uber had braved the weather and miraculously made it there, so the spa ladies had to hurriedly pack up. I was surprised they had shown up in the first place.

I grabbed a bottle of sparkling water. I needed to pace myself with the drinking if I wanted to make it through the night. I stood by the window and looked outside. In the background, I could hear Parry and Riya talk about the dinner menu and planning how to time the courses.

I saw a car pulling up in front of the building and was shocked to see Naina getting off. I had hoped she would make it, but deep down, I didn't think she would actually show up. All the cat-and-mouse games and near-misses in the lead-up to this evening had made me sceptical. But seeing her now, I felt both relieved and excited about finally getting some answers from my dearest friend.

11

Instead of straightaway making her way upstairs, I saw Naina walk towards a shed and stand underneath. She pulled out her phone, and I immediately felt my phone buzzing. I looked behind me and noticed that Parry and Riya were still in deep conversation. Whatever it was Naina wanted to talk to me about, she did not want anybody else to be privy to our conversation. Instead of answering the phone, I replied via text: 'Coming down'.

I was just about to exit the room when Parry spotted me. 'Maya, need anything?' he asked.

'No, all good. I just need to grab something from my room.'

I stealthily made my way out of the apartment and took the elevator downstairs. It was pouring and I ran towards the shed. But there was absolutely no sign of Naina there. I dialled her number and could hear her phone ringing. I tried to identify where the sound was coming from and narrowed it down to the basement garage. I walked towards the garage, her ringtone getting louder. Lying in front of a storage unit, I found Naina's phone discarded. I picked it up and noticed it was a password-protected iPhone 8.

Damn it. I was starting to get worried about Naina. As much as I wanted to avoid being pessimistic, I couldn't help but pray that nothing bad had happened to her. This weekend was turning out to be a lot stranger than I had imagined, and Naina had a huge part to play in that.

I was about to turn back and leave when I spotted a shadow.

'Hey!' I called out loudly. The person ran towards the building without turning around, even though I was pretty sure they had heard me. Could that have been Naina? As the figure passed from under the streetlight, I noticed it was Devi. I called out to her, but I could no longer be sure she could hear me—it had started raining heavily again.

A doorstopper had been placed to give me access to the building, but I didn't have the elevator code. I looked at the staircase and sighed and started climbing up. Thankfully, I was in somewhat decent shape. When I reached upstairs, it looked like nothing had changed. Everybody was cosily lounging around in the living room. There was no sign of Naina. I looked for Devi, and she was neither in the kitchen nor her room. I almost wanted to go and tell Riya to send out a search party. I went to the window and saw the car that Naina had stepped out of backing out. Was it possible she got cold feet and decided to leave? The thought sent a shudder down my spine. Why would she play such games? I was so close to seeing her, and now there was a chance she had left without even meeting us.

I joined the others dejectedly, deep in my thoughts.

'While we are waiting for Naina, do you guys want to know how Riya found out I was gay? It was probably one of the most embarrassing moments of my life,' Parry said.

'That sounds like a fun story. Go ahead, Riya, spill the beans,' Sam said. I was glad the focus was now on Parry, and I could zone out. I was feeling very queasy and couldn't be at peace till I knew Naina's whereabouts.

'I was out with friends one night, getting pizza, and lo and behold, I saw two men making out in a booth at the back. They were told off by the waitress a couple of times, but they ignored her. Something ticked me off about their entitled behaviour. My friend's ten-year-old daughter was also with us. I am not a prude, but I do believe in appropriate public behaviour, so I went over and just as I was about to give them a piece of my mind, one of them turned out to be good ol' Parry. His expression was priceless, and I almost wanted to laugh,' Riya said. 'Without saying a word, I just went back to our table. My friends were just about to leave when Parry quickly came and asked me if I would have a drink with him so he could explain himself. I was reluctant, but I also did not want to shrug him off. I knew what it was like to be shrugged off and have people behave like you did not exist. So we walked over to the bar; I ordered a glass of Chenin Blanc and Parry ordered a glass of sparkling water with lots of lemons in it. Strange choice, as I expected him to order a drink—he needed the liquid courage, after all. But I bet he wanted to keep his head clear for whatever he was about to share with me.

'Before he could begin, I put my hand over his and told him it was okay, and that it really wasn't a big deal. Yug would, at times, make homophobic comments, so I advised Parry that it might be a good idea to ease him into this, and he agreed,' Riya said.

'I was relieved Riya knew and grateful that she had been so accepting. Even though in big cities like Delhi and Mumbai, being gay is more acceptable, I've grown up in a small town where it is simply unheard of. Even today, if I ever decide to come out to my mother, she will probably need to be explained what it even means to be gay as it would go way beyond her comprehension. Like it is beyond Yug's comprehension,' Parry said.

'Well, Yug is not homophobic, per se. I just think he has a bigger issue with my closeness to you rather than with you being gay,' Riya said.

The two of them were so engrossed in their own conversation that Sam and I needn't even have been there. At some point, they decided that Riya's make-up had to be touched up and left the room. I was alone with Sam.

'So Sam, what's it like being back in India?'

'Not bad. I'm here only for a few days before I head back to London. Zayn's parents are visiting from Pakistan, so I have my work cut out for me. Chop chop.'

'I can imagine. Did you have a chance to meet your family here in Delhi?'

'Well, after I decided to marry Zayn, they pretty much disowned me. This is what happens when you follow your heart, Maya. Sometimes I wonder if it was even really worth it. Life has not always been easy with Zayn.' She was looking at her cocktail, gently swirling it. 'I haven't seen my parents in so many years, coming here brings back so many memories. You know when my uncle passed away, I wasn't even allowed to attend his prayer meeting. The reason given was that I had married a Pakistani and since he retired as an army general, it might disturb his old retiree friends. That was it. I decided I really needed to move on with my life and stop clinging to straws,' she said.

'I am sorry to hear that. It must have been difficult.'

'No, you aren't, and neither is Naina. This is a classic case of "I told you so". And you know what? You girls were right and I was wrong. Because marrying Zayn was the worst decision of my life. He just wasn't who I imagined him to be. I embraced his culture, his family and what did I get in return? Nothing, zilch. He can't even hold down a job. I am just so exhausted.'

'Well, we all make mistakes and trust me, nobody has made more mistakes in life than I have. And you know very well that my issues with Zayn had nothing to do with him being Pakistani. I just disliked him and felt you could have done so much better. But in retrospect, I realise it wasn't really my place. You are an intelligent, thinking adult, and I should have supported you instead of throwing a wrench in your plans.'

'It's fine, Maya. Don't beat yourself over this. I am not leaving Zayn any time soon—we have the girls to think about. However, what I am glad about is that you and I have finally been able to put our petty differences aside and move on.'

Sam came over to me and we hugged. I was glad we had made up. I couldn't wait to meet Naina and set things right. Riya had rejoined us, as had Parry, and I had become wholly preoccupied with Naina.

'Girls, there is something I need to talk to you about.' Before I could say anything more, the doorbell rang.

12

We heard footsteps and saw Naina entering the living room. The wait was finally over. She looked just the same. She was wearing a flowing oversized white dress that reached up to her knees and a light denim jacket with Converse sneakers, and her hair was flowing down her back. She could have been a model for Free People in her bohemian chic look. She wore only a necklace with a pendant and light eyeliner, along with a light pink lip gloss. Even though Naina was around my age, she looked a lot younger. There were no lines or creases on her face. I was pretty sure when Naina entered a room, people turned to look at her. She was blessed that with so little effort, she could look so good. I was glad to see no traces of anxiety or stress. And more importantly, I was relieved to learn Naina had not abandoned the idea of joining us.

We all rushed over to greet her. Naina hugged us, and I noticed we all got a little teary-eyed. So many memories came flooding back.

'OMG, I can't believe that the four of us are back together under one roof. This is just so wonderful,' Naina said.

Her frantic messaging had made me think she wouldn't look this cheery. She did not look like a person going through any kind of emotional upheaval. Maybe I was reading too much into the situation, but I also knew that I would not be able to rest until I asked Naina and got to the bottom of why she had been trying to reach me.

'Naina, you look the same. You haven't aged one bit,' I said.

'Oh come on, Maya. You look great, too,' Naina said modestly.

'I got your message when I arrived, but for some reason, I wasn't able to reach you when I tried. Anything you wanted to talk about? All good, I hope?' I asked.

'Glad you brought that up. I was only trying to reach you as I know how you get, Maya, and I did not want any awkwardness between us to ruin Riya's fortieth. I thought we should talk before we met in person and catch up. That's it,' Naina said.

Even though Naina said it in a casual, nonchalant way, I knew her well enough to know that there was more to it. But I let it pass for the time being. Clearly, whatever it was, she wasn't going to talk about it in front of everybody else.

'Ladies, no heavy stuff tonight. I have the perfect evening planned for us. Let today be all about fun, memories and, of course, me,' Riya said.

'Which is why I have here a tray full of champers for you lovely ladies.' Parry walked in carrying a tray.

'That would be great, and as usual, Parry, you read my mind,' Riya said.

'What's with these pyjamas you girls are wearing?' Naina asked, trying to stifle a smile.

'Parry, can you give Naina her swag bag? We don't want her to feel left out now, do we?' Riya said.

Parry walked in carrying a brown paper bag and handed it over to Naina. She pulled out the same pyjamas as the rest of us and burst out laughing.

'Do you really expect me to wear this?' Naina asked.

'Of course, I do. Aren't we all?' Riya said.

'Well, okay. I don't want to ruin the fun so I will be a sport and wear it. Can someone show me to my room?' Naina said.

Riya called Devi in, and she led Naina down the hallway to show her where her room was.

While Naina went to change, Riya excused herself to check up on Bella. Sam wanted to use the restroom, so she left as well. I was standing alone in the living room, looking at Riya's artwork on the wall. I always wondered what interested people about abstract art—was it the freedom of interpretation? I went over to the side table where their family photos were on display. She and Yug looked young and very happy, and you could tell these photographs were taken during happier times. I spotted a picture of the four of us at Central Park. I pulled it out and brought it close to my face to inspect. I noticed all of us were looking straight at the camera, except for Naina. She hated having her pictures taken and made it a point to never cooperate. We called her the 'photobomber'.

It then struck me—why not talk to her right now? She was alone, and I could speak to her in the privacy of her room. Once we had settled our issues like Sam and I had, we could enjoy the rest of the evening in peace together. At some level, I was also disturbed by my conversation with Dhruv on the flight here. For her to want to take her own life was a huge thing, and I needed to understand what had made her do it. She may have brushed off my attempts to reach her as something casual, but I knew there was more to it. Her behaviour was a little odd, and even if I was overreacting, I wanted to hear it straight from the horse's mouth.

I walked towards the room Naina was staying in. There seemed to be nobody inside—it was dark and the night light had been turned on. I noticed a notepad and pen. I wrote a quick note to Naina and then remembered I had her phone on me. I pulled it out of my pocket and placed it on her bedside table. Naina had always been a little scatterbrained, so it wasn't all that surprising if she had dropped her phone without realising it. I was about to leave when I heard a hanger drop in the closet. I was about to walk towards it when I heard muffled voices from the bathroom. Before I could knock on the door, I heard two voices—Sam had beaten me to it. I was about to turn around and leave when I heard something that made me stop in my tracks.

'Sam, can you please not mention anything to Maya? I really don't want to create a scene,' Naina pleaded.

'I will not, Naina, but you do have some explaining to do,' Sam said.

'Well, I had nowhere to go at that time of the night. I was low on cash. Not one of my proudest moments, and I am very ashamed. Besides, a lot has changed since then. I can assure you that where I am right now in life, it will not happen again,' Naina said.

'For heaven's sake, Naina, do you hear yourself? You are a literal princess—you have been fortunate enough to have studied at some of the best institutions in the world, but in your hour of need, you checked into a homeless shelter instead of a hotel or reaching out to one of your friends, who would have been more than willing to help you out? Something just doesn't feel right,' Sam said.

'Shhh … can you keep your voice down?' Naina said, and she walked towards the door and shut it tighter.

I was a little taken aback by what I had overheard. Homeless shelter? Naina? Sam knew what was going on but was not going to disclose it—what was happening? I almost felt like things were deliberately being hidden from me.

I was about to turn around and leave when I jumped up in fright.

'A penny for your thoughts?' Parry said, having caught me eavesdropping, red-handed. How long had he been standing there? I was a little embarrassed.

'Oh sorry, I was checking in on how long the girls were going to take. Where's Riya?'

'She's still with Bella. Want to go see her? It's beautiful seeing them together.'

'Sure. By the way, Parry, what were you going to say earlier? About Yug?'

'Oh, silly me, nothing really. I tend to exaggerate things sometimes. Yug's great but like all metrosexual straight men, he can be a pain in the you-know-what. Oh, look there's Riya.'

We'd stopped outside Bella's room, and Parry had opened the door slightly for me to look inside. Riya was in a rocking chair with Bella in her arms. There was a look of contentment and satisfaction on her face. She was singing softly to the baby, rocking her back and forth. She seemed so immersed in a world of her own, I was glad that she had found the happiness she so deserved.

'Shall we go back to the living room, Parry?'

We returned to the living room; Sam and Naina were already there. The tense atmosphere I had witnessed earlier was long gone. So whatever it had been, Sam and Naina seemed to have resolved it. That was the thing about being good friends; it was easy to bury the hatchet and move on.

'So where have you been all this while, Naina?' Sam asked.

'Well mostly in San Francisco, with the occasional trip to New York,' Naina said.

'Why didn't you ever call me if you were in New York? It would have been great to see you,' I asked her, accusingly.

'Well, I hadn't been in touch for such a long time, I just felt awkward reaching out. Besides, I have come only a handful of times, and that too on super quick trips.'

'Oh, you know, I met Dhruv on the flight here.'

'Dhruv? Which one? Khanna?' Naina asked.

'Yep, the same.'

'What is he doing in New York?' Sam asked.

'He works for a consulting firm, so he keeps coming to New York. I told him to reach out when he is visiting next. In fact, he was asking about all of you.' I was carefully observing Naina while talking about Dhruv. I was hoping to see some kind of reaction or change in her expression, but she was poker-faced. I knew there was more, but like all other things, I let it pass for tonight. Now was not the time to rake up old issues.

'Enough with the interrogation, Maya. Tell us about your hot dating life, Naina! Being single and all that,' Riya asked, walking back into the living room with a glass of red wine in her hand.

I could tell the alcohol was kicking in and this was the fun Riya. But if she didn't hydrate enough or get some food in her belly, we would be seeing a different side to Riya tonight, and experience had taught me that was not a pretty sight.

'I have been in a relationship for some time now. But our relationship is complicated. We keep breaking up and getting back together, but this time, I think we will see it through. Actually, I am almost certain we will,' Naina said optimistically.

'What's his name? Where is he from? Deets, please!' Sam said.

'Ladies, slow down, I have only just arrived. How about we get me a bit drunk before we talk?'

'Okay then, moving on to you, Maya. A successful, hot lawyer like you. How many hearts have you broken?' Sam asked.

'Well, I have dated on and off but nothing serious, really. And of course, my marriage,' I said. Usually, I kept mum about that rather inconsequential phase in my life with the weasel. But I think being around close friends and letting my hair down—and, of course, the alcohol—was kicking in and helping me open up. It felt good to just be myself and not feel judged.

'No way. Married to whom? How come I never got to read about this fab marriage on Page 6?' Sam said.

'Well, it was really short-lived. The guy turned out to be a really controlling, cheating creep. So I called it off. We had an amicable divorce, and that's it.'

'Amicable? That sounds awfully mature,' Riya said.

'Well, amicable in the sense we both wanted to get out of it ASAP. But I am pretty sure if both of us are put in the same room, only one of us will walk out alive,' I said, taking a sip from my champagne flute.

The next thing I knew, Riya took her champagne flute off the table and smashed it on the ground. 'To new beginnings!' she announced.

Sam followed suit and then Naina, hesitating, which left only me. I followed them, too. It felt like a release. We all stood there looking at the broken shards and started laughing.

'As the old German saying goes, shards are supposed to bring luck,' Riya said.

'Now that you are a hot single divorcee, are you dating again or have you become a workaholic?' Naina asked.

'I wouldn't say that. Yes, work is a huge part of my life and has always been my number one priority. That is actually why some girls from my work thought I should learn to let loose once in a while and made me join this dating app called Coffee Meets Bagel. I went on some interesting dates, but nothing ended up being serious,' I said.

'Isn't there a saying you have to kiss a few frogs before you meet a prince? Besides, I think, Maya, you are really having the last laugh. I have been married for several years now, and I would love to be in your shoes any day over that,' Sam said.

'Well, the grass isn't always greener on the other side, Sam. I do sometimes miss not having a significant other and babies and all of that. It's not always easy coming home to an empty apartment and not having someone greet you after a rough day,' I said.

'Trust me, if you had a husband like Zayn, you're better off on your own,' Sam said, laughing.

We all laughed—by now, it was no longer a secret that none of us was particularly fond of Zayn.

'By the way, what are you doing nowadays, Naina?' Riya asked.

'I am writing,' Naina answered.

'You mean you left your dream job at a law firm to write?' Sam said.

'Yes, it just wasn't my passion. I took up the job more to clear my student loans and because it was what was expected of me. When you go to law school, write and pass the New York bar exam, you really don't have a choice but to practise law,' she explained.

'So have you written anything exciting? Some juicy novels under some exotic pseudonym?' I asked.

'Well, not really. I write an immigration blog. It's something super lowkey that I do in my spare time. Sort of a creative outlet without the hassle of co-workers and leaving the house.'

'You do know I work at an immigration law firm, right? I could have helped you promote your blog by spreading the word.'

'I know, but this was more a philanthropic exercise. I write an opinion piece on immigration and then take live questions. I wanted flexibility, and this allows me that. Some days, I write two blog posts a day, and on others, I don't write at all.'

'How many subscribers do you have?' Sam asked.

'Well, about fifty thousand,' Naina said modestly.

'That's awesome. Once we are done with dinner, the first thing I am going to do is have a look at your blog,' I said.

'If it's philanthropic, then how do you pay your bills? Have a sugar daddy or something? You don't exactly look like you are struggling,' Riya said drunkenly.

There was pin-drop silence in the room. It was one thing asking about a friend's dating life and a whole other thing to blatantly attack her character and claim she has a sugar daddy. Riya looked around, probably expecting us to laugh. But when she saw that nobody was amused, she immediately took it all back.

'I was kidding, guys. Can't old friends joke around? Are we all supposed to have filters?' Riya said dramatically with her hand on her chest.

Parry walked in and said, 'You are even more beautiful in person!'

'Excuse me?' Naina said.

'Sorry, I didn't introduce myself earlier. I am Parry, Riya's housekeeper/assistant/manny. I like to think of myself as being a jack *and* master of all trades! Pleased to meet you, Naina,' Parry said sassily.

We all started laughing; Parry had walked into the room at just the right time.

'Pleasure to meet you, too.'

'Has Riya told you about my artwork?'

'Come on, Parry. Stop!' Riya exclaimed.

'What kind of artwork? I have always been interested in art and would love to see your work. In fact, just an hour ago, I was admiring that beautiful abstract painting on the wall,' I said.

'You have already seen my work,' Parry said.

'Where?' I looked around the apartment. Riya had a lot of interesting paintings, sculptures and sketches displayed everywhere. I couldn't guess what Parry was referring to.

'She is my muse,' he said, pointing at Riya.

We all laughed, but I did feel like Parry was being sincere, and I was glad he had helped lighten the mood in the room. He took up a dustpan and started picking up the shards of glass off the floor.

'Okay ladies, attention. Before we all get super plastered, I had arranged for a photographer to come and take some shots of all of you and document Riya's special day. But it looks like there's a flood outside, and I don't want any of you to panic at this, but the building is inaccessible for the time being, at least until the water recedes. So I will serve as your photographer with my Polaroid camera here. I hope we can capture your priceless moments from tonight,' Parry announced.

The news about the worsening weather condition was worrying, but everyone seemed to be taking it in their stride, so I too let it go. Posing for photographs, however, was something I just wasn't in the mood for. 'Parry, do we really have to?'

'Come on, Maya. Be a sport. Do something spontaneous for once,' Riya exclaimed.

'Oh well, okay.'

Parry took some shots from various angles, and I had to admit, it was a lot of fun. We all huddled around to have a look at the photos. We all looked so happy, and then I saw it—Naina had her fists clenched in each and every picture. When I looked at her, she turned the other way and said something to Sam, deliberately not making eye contact with me.

'Talking about art and paintings reminds me, Riya, I would love to see that painting you were telling me about earlier, the one that's in your bedroom,' Sam said.

'Sure. Would you guys like to see it, too?' Riya asked.

'Actually, since I've arrived, we have all been so caught up with catching up, I haven't even had a chance to unpack. So can you excuse me, please?' Naina said.

I took this as a golden opportunity to get some one-on-one time with Naina. I could tell the evening was getting too much for her and that she needed a breather.

'Naina, maybe I could help you and that way we can catch up, too?'

'Sure.'

'Okay, ladies, so we will see you back here in a few,' Riya said, walking out of the room, Sam and Parry following her.

We reached Naina's room, and I closed the door behind us. I plonked onto her bed.

'How have you been, Naina?'

'I've been okay.'

'What happened? I don't mean to rake up all our issues, but I still can't understand why we lost touch.'

'There was a lot going on in those days, Maya. Even thinking about it makes me feel exhausted,' Naina said resignedly.

'Well, I am glad you made it here this weekend. I was a little worried about you. Especially since you had unsuccessfully tried reaching me on multiple occasions.'

Naina walked over to her bag and pulled out a notepad and pen. She scribbled a note and shushed me with her finger, so I wouldn't say anything.

'You know, Maya, I am so glad Riya arranged this weekend, and I was able to make it.' By now, Naina was standing in front of me. She handed the note over. It said: 'We need to talk. Not now.' I folded the note and put it in my pocket. I looked at Naina quizzically, and then I saw the dread in her eyes. I was about to open my mouth when she looked towards the door. I leaned over and gave her a hug. Whatever it was, it was something serious, and it was playing on Naina's mind. She wanted to talk to me but was scared someone would be listening in. We were all friends, and this weekend was a time for fond memories and familiarity. A safe space. But Naina did not seem to see it that way at all. The cause of her fear lay within these four walls. Unfortunately, so many years had elapsed since the last time we met that I didn't feel like I had the right to pester her for answers. We quietly made our way out of her room, and I felt an inexplicable heaviness, sadness—and fear.

13

'Glad you guys are finally here. I really wanted to show you something. A special surprise I had planned,' Riya said.

'Riya, you are full of surprises tonight,' Sam said.

We noticed Devi walk in.

'Yes?' Riya asked her.

'It's Bella Baby's bedtime,' Devi said.

'Guys, can you excuse me for a couple of minutes? I like to put Bella to bed. Mommy duties, you see,' Riya said.

'Of course. Need any help? I am great with babies,' Sam said.

'Thanks, but what you can do is have an extra drink on my behalf while I am away,' Riya said.

Naina looked up at us, questioning.

'In case you are wondering, Bella is Riya's six-month-old baby girl,' Sam said.

'Oh. She has a baby. That's a surprise. Did any of you know about this?' Naina said.

'No. Only got to know when we got here; she's a beautiful baby girl.'

'I am so happy for her. Didn't Riya always talk about wanting to have a baby?'

'She did, and I don't think she could have got a better fortieth birthday present this year than Bella.'

Riya joined us in the living room at this point. She took us all to her family room, which was outfitted with comfortable recliners, a popcorn machine and a wine cooler. I could tell the projector had been set up, and we were going to witness a cinematic extravaganza. Riya always went the extra mile, so this wasn't surprising at all.

I noticed Devi walk in with misshapen coffee mugs on a tray. I leaned over and took one. I looked at the contents and started laughing. The coffee mugs contained rosé. When we were in New York, we would often drink cheap rosé in the summer months, out of any mug we could get our hands on. We never kept any glassware because we would break them in no time. Mugs were just more durable and practical during our student life. Riya brought a big bowl of M&M's.

'You remembered,' Sam said, laughing.

'Of course, no evening was complete without M&M's, cheap rosé and a mindless chick flick and, of course, gossip,' Riya said.

I noticed Parry walk behind Riya with a smaller bowl of chocolate M&M's.

'Let me guess, that's for me, right, Riya? You remembered I have a peanut allergy,' Naina said.

We all sat down. I sat between Riya and Parry. The projector was turned on. Riya had thoughtfully compiled all our photographs from New York. There was one photograph of us at Central Park in the fall. We had bought wine and cheese from a local farmers' market and were all completely sloshed. We laughed at the memory. Then there were some more of us at Café Wha in the West Village, where we loved watching performances by up-and-coming comedians and artists. Finally, we reached our graduation pics. There was Sam and me in our robes during the ceremony, then another of Riya, Sam, Yug and me at Ai Fiori, getting dinner together. Only one person was missing from them—Naina.

We noticed the door of the room open and close. Riya instructed Parry to turn on the lights, and we noticed Naina had left the room.

'Maybe it was a bad idea to rake up old memories like this?' Riya said.

'No, it wasn't. You were only trying to be nice. Your heart was in the right place,' Sam said.

'Why do you think she left the room? I did not want to make anybody uncomfortable. I just wanted to relive old memories. Besides, when I planned all this, I wasn't even sure if Naina was going to come. And frankly, I felt that after so many years, the photos were harmless, and no one would be offended. Clearly, I was wrong,' Riya said.

'You are reading too much into it, Riya. It's your fortieth. Don't let something as small as this ruin the lovely weekend you have planned,' Parry said.

We got up and followed Riya back into the living room. Naina was sitting on a couch, looking out of the window. I could see her eyes were moist, and it was really sad to see her like this. A realisation hit me—we had all drifted so far apart that we had no idea about each other's struggles and sensibilities. After all the blood, sweat and tears that had gone into law school, maybe not attending her graduation had had a deeper impact on Naina than any of us had thought.

'Are you okay, love?' Riya asked her.

'Yes. Thank you for putting it all together, Riya, and my getting emotional had nothing to do with the photographs. It's the memories. So many of them, and they all remind me of a happier time in life,' Naina said.

'Naina, I know that's not true. Come on, out with it,' I said.

'Well, guys, I want to apologise for saying that watching those videos brought back memories that I wanted to erase forever. It's a reminder of me failing my family, you guys, the education I received and, most importantly, myself. I was weak, and there were circumstances that overpowered my decision to attend graduation. In retrospect, I probably should have attended,' she said.

'It's okay, Naina. You don't have to explain.'

I always knew it wasn't as simple as Naina having an emotional outburst around the graduation and deciding not to attend on a whim. Her issues ran far deeper, and she was pushed so far that she wanted to take her own life. But I knew I could only talk to her one-on-one about it. Riya and Sam were great, but we all had too much to drink, and Riya could get a little boorish, so I decided better to move past the subject for now.

Naina looked at me gratefully for not persisting and gladly changed the subject.

'Do you mind if I just wash my face and join you? I am quite a mess, aren't I?' Naina said.

'Would you like me to accompany you?' I asked.

'That would be great,' Naina said.

I walked down the hallway with her, and she held my hand tightly. I waited until we had reached her room and closed the door.

'Naina, what is going on? I didn't want to say anything outside in front of the others, but I can clearly tell that something is bothering you. And about graduation—you know I spoke to Dhruv, so I know exactly what happened that day. Since you gave me that note, I know for sure that something is bothering you and we need to talk about it *now*.'

'I know, Maya. Where do I even begin? My life is such a mess, and I just had to come here this weekend to set things right before it's too late. But I also know now is not the time to talk.'

'Late? As in? Is there an issue with your health? Please don't tell me you are terminally ill?'

'No, no. Of course not. Though I wish that was the case. I really need to speak to all of you together. But I knew I could only do it if you were going to be there, Maya.'

'What is the matter, Naina? I can help, you know. But for that, you will have to talk to me and share things candidly with me.'

'I am so, so scared, Maya. I don't know where to begin.' Naina tearily walked over to me, and I held her in a hug. Before we could resume our conversation, we heard a loud crashing sound. We quickly rushed out of her bedroom and noticed a vase in the corridor was lying on the floor, shattered. There was no sign of anybody else there. I suddenly heard footsteps and Parry rushed over to check on us.

'All well?' Parry asked, bending down and instinctively cleaning up the mess.

I knew the vase did not magically break on its own. Somebody had been eavesdropping on my conversation with Naina and, for some reason, didn't want me to hear what she had to say. Patience was not my thing, and the fact I couldn't get to the bottom of things was driving me nuts. But I also knew I needed to remain calm and composed because whatever it was Naina was scared of, the last thing I wanted was to put her life in jeopardy.

The only choice I now had was to wait for dinner to get over so I could try to talk to her again. I had to remember to drink less in order to think clearly.

I decided to grab a glass of water as hydration was a must. In a corner of the kitchen, I saw a chef sitting on a chair, watching a YouTube video about plating and nervously sipping a cup of green tea. I noticed he was sweating profusely and looked stressed out. I grabbed a glass of water and saw the trashcan overflowing with empty food containers. Clearly, the chef had no plans to cook tonight and had brought food from outside. Why was he not doing his job? He surely had some explaining to do.

14

'Girls, what do you think of my house? Fab, right?' Riya said.

I could tell Riya was getting hammered, and that was never a good idea. Especially since we hadn't even started with dinner as yet. Thankfully, Parry soon came and announced that dinner was ready. We all walked over to the dining table, and it couldn't have been set more beautifully. There were vases of every shape and size strewn all over the surface of the table. White candlestands all around, and Riya had laid out fancy dinnerware from Tiffany's, with crystal glassware from Baccarat and shiny silverware from Christofle. I saw on top of the credenza that there was a bottle of Dom Pérignon champagne uncorked and left to chill.

'I must compliment you, Riya, this is one beautiful table,' I said appreciatively.

'It's all Parry. He plans and conceptualises, while I just write out the cheques,' Riya said.

'Don't be so modest, Riya, you have groomed me, and I am who I am today, thanks to you,' Parry said.

'Same here,' she said and started laughing.

Naina joined us at the table. I noticed she looked a lot better after our conversation. But we had unfinished business, and the first opportunity I got, I needed to speak to her. Until then, I decided to guard her like a hawk.

I heard something crackle in the background; it was the baby monitor.

'Looks like it's time for Bella's feed,' Riya said getting up from the table.

'Don't worry, let me handle it. You enjoy yourself,' Parry said.

He got up and left, and we could hear him cooing over the monitor. Bella was no longer crying. He returned to join us, a couple of minutes later.

'Parry is such a godsend—I would be a total mess if it wasn't for him. He just takes care of everything,' Riya said.

'No, you wouldn't be a mess. You are stronger than you think you are. Never underestimate yourself, Riya. Look at all that you have accomplished and continue to,' Sam said.

I noticed Sam constantly kissed Riya's ass. Riya was more the outsider since she didn't attend school with the three of us, and so we were just not as close to her as we were to each other. But now, the dynamic seemed to have changed. Sam was constantly praising Riya, and while I had to admit she had definitely undergone a transformation in the last couple of years, it felt unnecessary to constantly applaud her.

And then, of course, there was Parry. But at least he was on her payroll, so it was part of his job description. I was starting to get a little annoyed at Sam—she had now started praising Riya for her impeccable fashion sense. I looked at Riya, and her eyes seemed like they were struggling to focus. The alcohol was definitely hitting her.

'Riya, you want some water?' I asked.

'The pot calling the kettle black, eh?' Riya said.

'Come on, Riya, let's not be nasty. We all know Maya had a couple of wild night-outs. But that was ten years ago! Maybe we should cut back on the jibes,' Naina chimed in.

'Sorry, Miss Perfect. I haven't been blessed with your flawless upper-crust upbringing, so I don't know what to say when. I am but a small-town girl who struck gold. Please forgive me for my atrocious manners,' Riya said, using a napkin and exaggeratedly wiping away something imaginary from her mouth.

I could sense the mood in the room getting tense. Riya was overreacting and there was no need for it. We had all been drinking, but she was clearly the worst at holding her liquor. Was it possible that she was under the influence of some kind of substance? She was, after all, taking those pills Devi had handed to her earlier.

'Well, I am starving. Where is that fancy meal you've been organising for us?' I asked. I then noticed there was one more person in a chef's outfit; he was the same guy I saw in the kitchen earlier. Without waiting for Riya, I signalled to him to come forward and join us. I wanted to get the dinner started as soon as possible before things got any more out of hand.

'Ladies, I am Chef Vik. I studied at the Institute of Culinary Education, and I have recently started curating dinners all over Delhi-NCR. I am super excited to be cooking for you lovely ladies tonight,' he said.

I took a gulp of wine and almost choked on it. More than a chef, he sounded like an actor. A bunch of middle-aged drunk women and a hot twenty-something guy? It didn't take much convincing. Only if I hadn't seen the empty food containers in the kitchen.

'Maya, are you okay? Need some water?' Naina asked with a look of concern on her face.

I nodded.

'What kind of food do you prepare?' Sam asked.

'Mostly, I curate menus for dinner parties. My guests give me guidelines, and I try to prepare meals as per their special requests.'

'What were the guidelines for this dinner?' Naina asked.

'Riya's guidelines were fairly simple. Since she said she was having a group of health-conscious ladies over, she wanted a healthy, wholesome farm-to-table dining experience. So my main goal with this dinner was to source healthy ingredients. I visited a local farm and sourced some fresh organic produce and let them do the talking, with very little involvement from my end.'

'That sounds delicious, Chef Vik. How about a drink for the road, ladies, before we begin the feast?' Parry said.

'Brilliant idea. A round of shots, perhaps?' Riya said.

'I think I will pass on the shots. But thanks anyway,' I responded.

'Should we all sit by the fireplace and chat for a bit? I feel like once dinner is served, we will get too busy eating and then before we know it, we will all go to bed, and boom, the night's over. I want this night to never end,' Riya said.

I noticed that with Riya, people could never really have their own opinion. One generally just went along with whatever she wanted. It also had to do with age. Riya was a couple of years older than us, so while we were at NYU, we all looked up to her, in a way, and willingly strung along with whatever she proposed. That pretty much set the course of our friendship.

We all followed her to the electric fireplace. It had seemed unnecessary when I first saw it, considering the tropical heat, but turned out to make for a cosy setting, thanks to the dip in temperature brought on by the storm. There was a long leather couch and two ottomans facing the fireplace. I sat on one end of the couch and Naina on the other. Sam took one of the ottomans, and Riya continued to stand.

Parry brought over a tray of Japanese whisky. We all took our crystal glasses and sipped quietly. I noticed Naina did not touch her drink. Instead, she gently placed it on a side table.

'Naina, I don't want to make this awkward, but we need to know what happened on graduation night, five years ago. You just disappeared.' I was shocked at Sam's ambush. She had always been the tactful one, but something had changed over the years.

'Well, as you know, I have my regrets about not attending the ceremony. But a lot was going on in my life at that time, and I just couldn't make it.'

'Like what?' Riya asked.

'I was in a relationship with someone, and it wasn't working out.'

'The same person you mentioned earlier? Why did you not talk to us about it?' Sam asked.

'It's complicated. Our relationship has been complicated from day one. Sometimes, I feel moving on would be the best thing for me to do. But I just can't envision a future without him.'

'Who is this mystery man?'

'I would rather not talk about him. At least not until we have figured things out.'

'Is it Dhruv Khanna? He always had the hots for you,' Riya asked.

'No, no. Dhruv has always just been a friend. He's fantastic, but I never had any romantic interest in him.'

'Tell us, Naina. We want to know,' Riya pressed.

I could tell Naina was getting uncomfortable, and Riya and Sam were hounding her.

'Guys, please stop putting her on the spot. She is an adult. If she wanted to tell us about him, she would have. Maybe she is scared one of us hotties will steal him away from her,' I said in an attempt to lighten the mood.

I also had another motive for changing the topic. I knew more about Naina's mystery man than I had let on, which is why it was imperative that I talked to her alone.

On the night before our graduation ceremony, I was about to fall asleep when I heard the gentle click of the door. I woke up with a start and noticed there was nobody in the room. I walked out of my bedroom and scanned the tiny living room to see if anybody was hiding in a corner. But I was alone and safe. I walked to the window and looked down. I saw a person emerging from our apartment building and heading towards the opposite side of the street. It was Naina, and she was carrying an umbrella; there was a slight drizzle. I watched as she hurriedly crossed the street and joined a man there; he was waiting for her. I couldn't make out who he was, and the big golf umbrella soon concealed them both from my sight. I stood at the window for a couple of minutes, watching as she crossed the street and re-entered the building. Sam had been asleep through all this, and I didn't want to wake her up. I was convinced that there was more to this secret rendezvous and decided to confront Naina the next morning. Except, she disappeared before I had the chance. It had taken ten years for me to finally get another opportunity, and I wasn't going to let it go.

15

We all sat around the table. Riya was sitting at the head of the table, Sam and Naina were sitting together on one side, and Parry was seated next to me on the other. Parry opened a bottle of Bordeaux that he poured into a carafe. He swirled the wine and sniffed it and gave a satisfactory nod before leaving it to breathe.

'For a small-town girl, I have done quite well for myself, haven't I?' Riya said, looking around the room.

'What small-town girl? With your looks and body, you could give Gigi Hadid a run for her money,' Parry said.

'Parry, you really have no filter.'

We all started laughing.

'I have never asked you this, but how did you and Yug end up together?' I asked.

'End up together? He's too good for me, right?'

'You know I didn't mean it that way. He's lucky to have you.'

'Well, I was nineteen years old and I was an air hostess. On one of my flights, I met Mr Yug Sharma,' Riya said.

'And?' Sam asked.

'Well, like they say, the rest is history,' she concluded.

'Looks like someone here does not want to share their love story with us,' Parry teased.

'Oh, very well. We got talking, and Yug followed me to the staff area. I shared my phone number with him, and a couple of days later, he called me,' Riya said.

'I heard something about a "mile high club" kind of situation,' Naina said jokingly.

'Of course, you did. You and your ilk think Yug is too good for me, right? I don't deserve him? Guess what, you all have it wrong. Nobody even knows half the truth,' Riya said tearily.

'Come now, Riya. I don't think Naina meant it that way,' Parry said in an attempt to placate her. 'Look, Chef Vik is bringing in the first course now. Darling, let me fix your make-up so you look fab for those pics we are going to take tonight to post online.'

'I am sorry if I offended you, Riya. I only said it in jest,' Naina looked mortified.

Parry was making sense, and I was almost grateful for his presence. I did, however, think Riya had overreacted. I had no idea she had such a deep-rooted inferiority complex. Why did she get so testy and pounce on Naina?

Chef Vik entered the room carrying two plates. We could now focus on dinner. I wanted it to be over quickly so I could spend time with Naina. By the looks of it, Riya was too drunk and was going to pass out very soon. As for Sam, she seemed quite distracted and in her own world, while Parry was just being himself.

'Ladies, I would like to present before you lemon sorbet with a splash of vodka. Hope this cleanses your palates before we start,' the chef said and left the room.

He re-entered with Devi a couple of minutes later. They cleared the table and when Devi bent down to collect my plate, she glanced at me discreetly. She was really odd. Now that I thought about it, Riya's entire household staff was rather strange.

Chef Vik walked in to place the next course on the table. I looked at what was put before me. On the plate were three golgappa shells and inside, I spotted what looked like shrimp ceviche. Chef Vik had artistically drizzled some red, green and brown sauce on the plate. I noticed everybody popped the whole thing into their mouths, so I did the same. Chef Vik was extremely talented in assembling good food. The whole thing was exploding with flavour and was indeed delicious.

As I was savouring the burst of flavours, I noticed Naina clutch the side of the table. Her face started to turn red and she was gasping for breath. It seemed like she was choking on something.

'Naina, Naina, are you okay?!' I asked. Her eyes were watering, and her pupils were losing focus. I rushed to her side while Sam tried to offer her water. I looked around for her EpiPen. I suspected she was having some kind of an allergic reaction. Her face had now turned alarmingly red.

Trying to temper the rising hysteria, I screamed, 'Can someone go to Naina's room and grab her EpiPen? I think she's having an allergic reaction. Hurry up!'

Sam rushed to locate the life-saving EpiPen while I tried to recall the little I knew about what to do in emergency situations and lay Naina on the floor, turning her on her side. She was clawing at her throat, struggling to breathe, and I could see her tongue swelling up, causing me to panic. Sam came rushing back, empty-handed. The EpiPen was nowhere to be found. Naina's eyes were rolling back, and I could tell she was losing consciousness.

As Riya, Parry, Sam and I crowded around Naina, she suddenly stopped moving. Shell-shocked, I checked her pulse as I suspected the worst. She was dead!

PART II

‘I am like an onion. You can peel away my layers, but the further you go, the more I’ll make you cry.’

16

'Maya, what the hell just happened?' Riya screamed.

'Naina is dead! OMG, I think she's actually dead!' I said, crouching beside Naina's lifeless body. I felt tears streaming down my face, and my vision starting to get blurry.

'What? Dead? How?!' Riya looked like she was going to pass out. Within moments, Parry reached her side and helped her to a nearby couch. He then handed her a bottle of water.

'Somebody needs to call an ambulance,' said Sam, her voice relatively calm. I saw her reach out for her phone and dial.

A short conversation later, she held out the phone to me. 'Nobody can come to us because of the storm. When I gave them Riya's address, they said it is one of the worst-hit areas, and it might be several hours before they get here. All the roads are flooded. Maya, they say they need someone to check for a pulse.'

I gingerly took the phone from her and spoke to the doctor at the other end. I told him what had happened. The dinner, Naina gasping for breath and choking, the lack of a pulse. On his directions, I again checked for signs of life, hoping with all my heart. But there were none. The doctor instructed me to hang up and call the police, assuring me they'd send over an ambulance the minute the roads cleared.

The call with the police was similar. They had no way of reaching Riya's building and suggested we leave the body untouched until they could get here, which could very well be a couple of hours from now.

'This house is now a crime scene,' I repeated what they'd said, the words chilling me to the bone.

Sam lost her composure and burst out crying. I went over and held her in my arms. She was shaking, and I felt a sadness descend over me. I held her close and we separated only after a few minutes had passed. I started picking on my cuticles. I needed some kind of a release—until Riya interrupted my thoughts. She looked a little more composed now.

'We could call Dr Arik to come check on Naina. He lives here, in this apartment building. Parry knows how to reach him,' Riya said.

'That's a great idea, Riya. Can you call him, Parry?' I said.

'He's an ob-gyn for high-risk patients. I will go get him right away. I think I saw him earlier this evening, which means he might still be at home. Let me go fetch him. I will be right back,' Parry said.

'That sounds like a good idea. Having a doctor examine Naina and, more importantly, document what happened would be advisable,' I said.

We all moved to the living room in silence, shaken up by the experience. We sat down as Naina lay on the ground just a few feet away from us. Just a couple of minutes ago, Naina had been alive and kicking at the dinner table, and now she was dead. The worst thing was that I had never had an opportunity to talk to Naina and would never know what she wanted to share with me. We would always have unfinished business.

'How in the world did this happen? Was she sick or something?' Sam asked.

Parry came back to the apartment with a tall and slender man wearing spectacles. He nodded in our direction and went straight towards Naina. Like a professional, he checked her pulse and did some preliminary examinations.

'Her body is still warm. Did she die just now?' Dr Arik asked.

'That's right,' Riya said. 'We sat down for dinner, and she seemed all right until she had the shrimp ceviche course. We all had it, and none of us got sick, other than Naina.'

'After she had the ceviche, what happened?'

'Well, she started choking and turning red, and soon after that, she got breathless and collapsed,' Sam said.

'Well, I can't say for sure, but based on my limited understanding of the situation, this looks like a case of asphyxiation.'

We all silently listened to his diagnosis.

'Was she allergic to anything?' Arik asked.

'Peanuts. Chef Vik, who prepared the dinner tonight, explained the full details of the dish before we all consumed it, and I distinctly remember him not mentioning peanuts. We've all been friends for a long time, and we all know about Naina's allergy. In fact, earlier tonight, we all had peanut M&M's except for Naina, who had the chocolate ones. We all knew how fatal her allergy could be,' Riya sounded more composed now.

'So, my understanding is that it happened right after she consumed the dish. Hmmm. Well, first of all, I suggest nobody touches Naina's plate until the authorities get here. We don't want to, in any way, tamper with evidence. I suggest we let the police come and investigate the matter further. I can see you ladies have been through enough already tonight. Perhaps a good idea would be not to speculate and put yourselves through hell.'

Riya went and lay down on the couch, closing her eyes. She was clearly distraught. Parry was sitting by her side, attending to her. I was still in shock but was able to function on autopilot with Arik.

We heard a loud crashing sound. Sam, Arik and I rushed out of the room towards the source of the sound. We noticed Chef Vik was sitting on the floor; his hands were shaking violently, and he was trying to clean the floor where he had dropped a glass platter. I noticed he had pierced his hand with the glass, but he was indifferent to the pain and there was blood gushing all over the white tiled floor. Devi was standing there with a sullen expression in a corner, not doing anything at all.

'Are you okay, chef?' I asked.

He did not respond. It seemed like his eyes were transfixed by the broken shards of glass. I bent down and put my arm around him.

'Stand up, please. Devi, do you have a first-aid kit lying around somewhere?' I asked.

Devi nodded and left the kitchen to go get it.

'It wasn't my fault. I am not responsible for Ms Naina's death,' the young chef said.

I wanted to reassure him, but I held back. How could this have happened?

Devi returned with the first-aid kit. Dr Arik promptly cleaned and dressed Chef Vik's hand. Sam and I returned to the living room to join Riya and Parry. I noticed Riya was curled up on the couch in a fetal position and had gone off to sleep. Parry was gently massaging her feet.

I went to the dining table, where less than an hour ago, we had been enjoying a lovely dinner together. I went over to Naina's chair and looked down at the contents of the plate. There seemed to be no trace of peanuts in there. I bent down and sniffed, but I couldn't smell anything funky. It still looked like shrimp ceviche in a golgappa shell. Peanuts had a distinct smell that couldn't be missed and it was clear this dish had no peanuts. Naina had consumed exactly what we all had. Except, we were all alive, and she was lying dead on the floor. My thoughts were interrupted by someone standing behind me. I turned around and saw Dr Arik.

'Have you called the police?' he asked, looking at me disapprovingly as only a couple of minutes ago, he had told us not to touch Naina's plate, in case the police saw it as tampering with evidence.

'We called an ambulance and the police, but with the storm raging outside, they said nobody could come right away. That is why we thought of calling you, in case there was any chance of reviving Naina … the slimmest chance. But I guess we were too late,' I said.

'If Naina had a known allergy, didn't she have an EpiPen or something?' he asked.

'She always carried one. But when we went to check her bag, she didn't have one today.' Something wasn't adding up here. We knew there was no saving Naina from her peanut allergy without the EpiPen. Naina could forget anything but her EpiPen. She once told me about how accidentally she had consumed soup that had peanuts in it, and the people she was with were unaware that she had an allergy. She had to be rushed to the emergency room in the nick of time, and that's how she was saved. After that day, she made it a point to always confirm if something had peanuts in it and carry her EpiPen along at all times. So where was it when she needed it the most?

'How do you guys know this lady? Have you informed her next of kin?' Arik asked.

Riya was now wide awake and looked a little more composed. 'Well, we are all very old friends, and it is my fortieth birthday today. We'd all gathered to celebrate together.' The initial shock and alcohol were both wearing off.

'Should we cover her with something?' Parry asked.

'That's probably a good idea,' I agreed.

Parry went over and covered Naina with a floral bedspread. A phone started ringing.

'Sorry guys, I have been expecting this call. If you will please excuse me. If you need anything at all, please let me know. You know where to find me,' Arik said.

'Thanks a lot for coming by,' Riya said.

With that, Arik left.

We all sat down in silence. We were all immersed in our own thoughts, still processing the sudden loss. Life would never be the same now that Naina was gone. Parry offered to bring some strong coffee so we could all clear our heads, especially after all the drinking. I looked at the floral bedspread and thought about Naina's body underneath it. Upon closer inspection, I noticed there were tiny daffodils all over it. Her favourite flower.

17

We were all speechless. Riya, Sam and I sat down on a couch, holding hands. Naina's lifeless body was lying in the adjacent room. It all seemed so surreal.

'How is it even possible, losing Naina like this?' Sam asked.

'Do you think she might have taken her own life?' Riya asked.

'What makes you think that?' I asked.

'I mean there is a strong possibility she did. There was something amiss about Naina tonight, even when I went to speak with her. She seemed fearful, neurotic almost, and maybe that's what pushed her to take her own life? But the only thing that bothers me about all this is why would she choose to do it in such a dramatic way? At the dining table, on Riya's fortieth birthday, and with all of us here. It just doesn't make sense.' Sam said.

'You are right, Sam. It's not Naina's style. She was one of the most modest people I knew, there's no way she would draw so much attention to herself like this,' I said.

'Are you trying to imply that someone killed her, then? Right here in my house? Under my watch? How ludicrous is that, Maya!' Riya said angrily.

'Riya, please don't jump the gun and overreact. We all are clearly disturbed, and I wasn't insinuating anything. We're just speculating what might have happened.'

'I need to go to the restroom.' Riya stood up and couldn't even stand straight, almost falling over. Sam immediately stood up to assist her out of the room. I remembered a time in my life when Naina had assisted me the same way.

She had stood by me when nobody else had. I scored the highest grades in each semester. Life was finally looking up for me. On one fun drunken evening, Naina and I were returning from a club, and we decided to stop over at the local 7-Eleven to pick up some candy, cigarettes and Cokes. Since I was buzzed, I popped some extra candy bars and cigarettes into my bag, thinking it would be a hoot and something we could laugh about later when we enjoyed our haul back at our apartment. The only thing I had not anticipated was that there was an off-duty cop in the next aisle. So after going through the checkout, as we were about to leave the store, Naina took my handbag from me. I tried arguing with her, but she insisted. When we left the store, the cop followed us out and confronted us. Naina had seen me 'shoplifting' and had also noticed the cop, who had been observing us very closely, so she decided to take the blame upon herself. Thankfully, the cop was a kind-hearted man and wasn't going to arrest us for stealing candy and cigarettes worth $12. Later on, when I asked her, she said I had more to lose than she did. That was the moment I knew that she was special, and our friendship was forever.

I never realised when tears started trickling down my cheek. For a change, I allowed myself to let it all go and grieve for the only true friend I ever had. I reflected on the conversation I had with her earlier and how she had feared for her life—I hadn't been able to help her out. It broke my heart that I wasn't able to be there for her.

I heard the clicking of heels; Sam joined me. She placed her arm around me. We both stood in silence. I heard a vibration somewhere in the background. Sam muttered something about Zayn calling her, and I was so deep in my thoughts that I never noticed she had left. I stood for a couple of minutes and then decided I wanted to search Naina's room for her EpiPen. We all might have missed it in our frantic search while Naina was having the allergic reaction. I entered her room and could still smell her perfume in the air, Penhaligon's Luna. I had to hold back my tears. I searched her room and the bathroom; her EpiPen was nowhere to be found. I noticed her jacket lying discarded on the bed. I placed my hand inside and noticed the phone I had found earlier, sitting in her pocket. I pulled it out, but it was switched off. I turned it on. I needed her fingerprint to access it. I was uncomfortable at the thought of going to Naina's lifeless body for this, but I knew I had no choice. I needed answers that would help me unravel exactly what happened to her. I noticed there was nobody in the living room where the body lay. Now was a good chance. I found a paper napkin; it would have to suffice, given the circumstances. I walked towards Naina's body, praying she would find the peace she so deserved. I pulled out her hand and pressed her thumb onto the phone. It unlocked immediately.

I took the cell phone and ran towards my bedroom. I glanced at the old iPhone. The first thing I did was to add my own thumbprint to unlock the phone. The only number stored was mine, and the only texts sent were to me. There were no photographs, emails or text messages other than that, which was odd because when I saw Naina waiting under the shed, I could have sworn she was talking to somebody on the phone. I noticed there was a Louis Vuitton overnight bag lying in one corner. I walked over and opened it. I found the usual stuff—a pair of pyjamas, a toiletry bag, a pair of slippers and a change of clothes. I dug deeper and noticed a flashlight and smiled despite myself. Naina was always scared of the dark. When I flung the flashlight back into the bag, I heard a rattling sound. I picked up the flashlight again and rattled it near my ear; there was something inside. I tried turning it on, but it wasn't working. There was only one AA battery inside instead of two. In addition to that, there was a SIM card. I pulled it out and noticed there was a pin too. My hands started to shake as I felt like I was about to uncover some dirty and dark secret about Naina. I shuddered and was almost tempted to go out and tell Sam and Riya about my discovery. But then I remembered Naina's scared face and something held me back. I took the pin and pulled out her SIM card. I placed the new one in and turned on Naina's phone. I unlocked it but nothing changed—it was still blank. Why did Naina have two SIMs if neither had anything on them?

I was about to give up all hope when the phone started vibrating.

'Hello,' I said. There was silence on the other end. I kept saying hello, but there was no response. I heard a faint sound in the background. The person on the other line hung up. I took a screenshot of the phone number and tried calling back, but it was switched off. There were too many mysterious things happening all around, and I needed to find out what the reason was. And where was that whirring sound in the background coming from? It sounded rather familiar.

I went to get a glass of water to clear my head. I entered the kitchen and noticed it was empty. I went to the refrigerator and pulled out a chilled bottle of Perrier and took a couple of sips. I noticed Chef Vik and Devi hanging out on the balcony, sharing a pack of *beedis* and a glass of scotch between them. I joined them, thinking it might be a good time to chat with them. I noticed Chef Vik looking ashen, and every time he took a puff, his hand shivered. Naina's passing had clearly shaken him up, and at some level, he held himself responsible. I noticed Devi, on the other hand, did not look as nervous, but there was something that was clearly bothering her. She kept glancing in my direction as if she wanted to say something to me.

Thankfully, Chef Vik excused himself, and I had Devi all to myself. I let him go; he was clearly in no state to talk.

'Devi, something bothering you?'

'No, Madam.'

'Okay. Because if there is something, you know you can tell me, and whatever you say here stays between us.'

She nodded. I knew she wanted to talk, but needling her right now was not the right thing to do. I was about to turn around and leave when I heard her approach me and slyly slip something into my hand. After this, she made a dash for it. I noticed she had put Naina's EpiPen into my hand. What was she doing with it? Was she trying to tell me that Naina's death wasn't an accident after all? I *had* to talk to her; it was important.

I knew where her room was. I knocked on the door a couple of times, and there was no response, but it was open. I walked in and closed the door behind me. The room was dark, and Devi was crying under her sheets. I went over and gently patted her on the back. She leapt up, and I told her to remain quiet. I did not want to attract any unnecessary attention. 'Devi, calm down, I only want to speak to you for a couple of minutes.'

She nodded. I noticed a water bottle lying on the table. I passed it to her, and she kept heaving and taking sips of water. I didn't want to push her any further until she had composed herself. Talking to her in this state would be pointless, but I also knew that what I needed to ask her couldn't wait—time was running out.

'Devi, this pen, where did you find it?'

'Madam, on the floor outside, in the corridor,' she said, not making eye contact with me.

'Listen, I know that's not true. Besides, you know this is a life-saving medicine, right? If we had found it in time, Naina would have been alive. So it's absolutely critical that you speak up and tell me where you found it.'

Devi made sure nobody was listening.

'Madamji, I found it in Bella Baby's crib. But only after Naina Madam was gone.'

'Crib?' I was a little surprised.

'Yes. I went to change Bella Baby's diaper, and in there, I discovered this pen. I thought it might be something expensive if someone had hidden it there. So I decided to keep it.'

'How on earth did it land in Bella's room?' I was confused by what I had just heard. I looked at Devi closely, and my legal training led me to believe that she knew more than she was letting on; she was being shifty. I would have to gently ease her into the conversation.

'Devi, you do realise this is evidence, and when the authorities come and I hand this over to them, questions are going to be asked about how I found it and where?'

I saw the blood drain from Devi's face.

'Madamji, there is one other thing I didn't mention.'

'Well, what is it?'

'I had gone to Naina Madam's room for turn-down service earlier in the evening. I saw her suitcase lying open and was curious to see what was inside. But then I heard someone at the door. So I hid in the closet in case they accused me of trying to steal something. I couldn't see who was outside as the lights were switched off, but they went straight towards Naina Madam's bag. I heard the zipper and then they left.'

'Okay.'

'I thought it was Naina Madam looking for something. But then a couple of minutes later, she herself entered the room and went straight to the bathroom, and Sam Madam followed her in.'

Now it made sense, the sound I had heard from the closet when I was in Naina's room.

'This is very helpful,' I told her.

'Thank you, Madamji. I won't get into any trouble, will I?'

'I hope not.' I didn't want to give Devi any false assurances and keeping her on her toes was in my best interest. I left Devi's room and found it unsettling that someone would want to hide Naina's EpiPen. Was it possible that she herself had hidden it so nobody could save her life? She had, after all, attempted suicide once before. It sounded very far-fetched.

I slipped the pen into my pocket and rejoined everyone else. We were still too shocked to say a word. Parry walked in a couple of minutes later, carrying a tray of steaming hot cups of coffee. I gratefully took a cup from him but a sadness had overcome me. Life could be so unpredictable. After years, I had been given a second chance to meet Naina, but she was gone.

'Do you think we could sit somewhere else? With Naina so close by, it just doesn't seem right,' Sam said, interrupting my thoughts.

'Sure, let's all go to my bedroom. I wouldn't mind stretching my legs a bit,' Riya said.

We entered a huge room. There was a California king-size bed littered with cushions that took up at least one-third of its surface, two nightstands, a sixty-inch television set and a couch. I noticed that Riya's nightstand had a bunch of things—pills, an eye mask, hand lotion and tweezers. But the side Yug slept on had nothing. It looked like nobody used the other side of the bed. The more I thought about it, the more it seemed like there was trouble in paradise.

Sam and Riya got into the bed, while I took the couch. Riya and Sam started crying, and I too couldn't help but get emotional. We all were mourning the loss of a dear friend. It was worse knowing that Naina had potentially tried taking her own life. Or had she? I did see Chef Vik plating in advance; anyone in the apartment could have sneaked peanuts into Naina's food. Since the plates were all labelled, the chef couldn't have caused the mix-up. But then, what if that person was Naina? Maybe she went and added peanuts to her own food before hiding her EpiPen. Given the circumstances, it seemed totally plausible. I should have discussed her suicidal tendencies with Sam and Riya earlier. Perhaps we could have talked to her or done something about it. But now it was too late.

I was always better at dealing with my emotions on my own. It likely had to do with being an only child and living on my own for so long. The fact that I hadn't been around when Naina had attempted suicide was already hard to come to terms with, but feeling like I had let her down; if perhaps I had been more involved in her life, I could have stopped her ... it was too difficult. I had lived a very hard life and let very few people in because I was fearful that they would let me down. I had let my guard down with Naina, but now that she too had left me, I knew that I would never be able to get close to anybody again. I knew that to cope with and accept Naina's passing, I had to talk to Sam and Riya. They would be able to help me because we all did, despite our differences, care deeply for each other, and if nothing else, our loss had only brought us closer.

'Guys, can we talk? There is something that has been bothering me for the longest time.'

'Sure,' Riya said.

'Parry, I would like to speak to Sam and Riya alone, if you don't mind.'

Parry immediately looked like a puppy dog at Riya, waiting for her to decide his fate. She nodded, and Parry left the room dejectedly. He would have loved to be a part of the drama.

'This is about graduation night.'

'What about it?' Riya asked.

'A lot changed that night. Naina vanished and Sam, you got married the next day.'

'So?' Riya asked.

'Did Naina reach out to either of you? We were very close, and it is strange she never tried to reach me again.'

I saw them exchange a knowing look.

'Well, she did,' Sam said.

'Are you saying she reached out to you?'

'Yes. I mean not exactly,' Sam said.

'When? And why didn't you call me?'

'Maya, hear yourself. How was I to call you? You were mad at me and mad at the world, and when you get that way, no amount of reasoning works with you. I called and left you many messages, but I never heard back from you.'

'Why did she call you?'

'To be clear, like Riya and you, I too was seeing Naina for the first time tonight after ten years. I was working at the South Asian Housewives' Movement, a shelter for victims of domestic abuse, where I was the project coordinator. My job was to review intakes once a week and decide how many women we were able to house. Many women would show up after a domestic squabble and go back to their husbands or partners the next day. We only allowed women whose lives were in serious danger. As I was going through the intake forms one day, I saw an application by Ms Naina Kumari with a photograph. I asked the coordinator for more details, but she said Naina had come for a few hours, and then, like many others, had left first thing, the next morning. There was no callback number or address on the sheet. So when I met Naina this weekend, I confronted her. She said she did not want to create any drama and forbade me from talking. Especially in front of you, Maya,' Sam said.

'Oh my God. Now it makes sense. I overheard you and her talking, and I thought you guys were hiding something from me. Do you know Naina overdosed on sleeping pills and tried to kill herself? I was on the flight to Delhi with Dhruv, and I was surprised when he told me this.'

'Yes, we do,' Riya and Sam said in unison.

Was I the only one wearing blinders?

'How did you guys know?' I asked.

'On the intake form, one had to mention health conditions. Naina had apparently walked into the shelter wearing a hospital ID bracelet around her wrist. Even though she was reluctant to share the details of her hospital visit with the intake coordinator, she had no choice,' Sam said.

'My goodness, this is just so sad. For Naina to have gone through all this on her own.'

'She could have asked for help. But she didn't. We must respect her reasons,' Riya said.

I nodded in agreement. Except, I knew deep down that that wasn't the case. Ten years had elapsed, and Naina was finally prepared to share her truth with me. And even though she was no longer alive, I wanted to make it my mission to find out what was it that had been bothering her in her final days.

18

'Riya, I don't feel great. May I be excused? I have a splitting headache, and I would like to take a bath as that might refresh me,' I said. I needed to get away from the mopey atmosphere in order to think clearly.

'Of course. Why don't you bathe in the master bedroom's bathroom? Parry will draw up a bath for you with my special Epsom bath salts. It will be good for your nerves,' Riya said.

'Thanks,' I said gratefully.

To enter the bathroom, you had to pass by a walk-in closet. Riya's closet was beautifully arranged and colour-coordinated. I saw a huge array of designer bags and shoes and a floor-to-ceiling mirror. In one corner of the room, I saw a mannequin on which was draped a complete outfit with coordinated shoes. There were accessories on a stand nearby. A pair of J Brand jeans, a white top and beige booties with simple gold jewellery and a Céline bag.

'Isn't that mannequin cool?' Parry said.

'It is. Usually only get to see those in stores.'

'You know what's special about this one? It's Riya's size; even its feet are the same size as Riya's. Perfection. Perfection. Perfection. That's what my Riya is all about. Took me six months to have this special mannequin delivered straight from Paris,' said Parry, gently stroking the mannequin like it was a prized possession.

'What's the purpose of this?'

'Well, Riya is very particular about her appearance. I put her look together the previous night, so she knows how it's going to look when she wears it the next day. And if for some reason—and this is *very* rare—the outfit needs tweaking, we do that so we don't waste any time the next morning when we have to do her hair and make-up,' he said.

'That's pretty amazing.' I suspected Parry was doing the exercise more for himself than for Riya. I was also a little appalled to hear that my friend was this particular about her appearance. Self-care was good and necessary, but I suspected she was setting punishingly high beauty standards for herself that were being fanned by Parry.

'Well, it would be amazing if Riya bothered to leave the house.'

'What do you mean?'

I could tell Parry regretted saying too much. But I had met enough people like him in my life to know that a little bit of praise could get their tongues wagging.

'Well, postpartum stuff. You aren't a mom, so you wouldn't understand.'

'Nor would you, for that matter, Parry.' I couldn't help but take a potshot at him; there was something so cocky and annoying about him.

We made our way into the bathroom. The flooring was off-white Calacatta marble, and I saw a jacuzzi that looked very inviting. I couldn't wait to soak myself in it.

I stood watching Parry dim the lights and light a few candles around the bathtub. He turned on the tap and then inspected the temperature. Once the tub was full, he turned off the tap and left the bathroom quietly, without saying a word to me. I stripped and got into the lukewarm water. It immediately relaxed my muscles. That relaxed feeling was short-lived as I could not really focus on it, knowing that Naina was lying in the adjacent room, dead and cold, while I was warm and comfortable and relaxing. I was having difficulty accepting she might have done it to herself. I put my head under the water and closed my eyes tight. When I tried to come back up, I felt a force pushing me down, and I started to suffocate. Was my life about to end just the way Naina's life had? I somehow managed to get my head out of the water and was left gasping for breath. I felt disoriented. I quickly got out of the water and wrapped a warm towel around my body. I saw no clothes but spotted a big, white fluffy bathrobe hanging on one of the walls. I wrapped it around myself and stepped out.

'Hey guys, will be back in a few minutes. Need to go change.'

'Of course, love.' Riya said.

I went back to my room and closed the door. I lay down on my bed for some time. The stress and the jet lag were getting to me. I stood up a couple of minutes later and changed into the first outfit I could get my hands on. Even though it was raining, I desperately needed some fresh air. I was in no mood to go back to Riya's bedroom and mope around with Sam and her. We all were grieving, and we all had different coping mechanisms. I stepped out of Riya's apartment and took the stairs to go down. Two floors below Riya's apartment, I spotted Dr Arik. He was smoking a cigarette on the landing and looking out at the rain. I suddenly felt a desperate need to smoke. I knew a few puffs would help me relax more than any amount of alcohol could.

'Mind if I bum a cigarette?'

'Of course.' He handed me a cigarette with a lighter. I lit it and took a few satisfying puffs.

'Quite a night, eh?' I said.

'Yes. I am sure it hasn't been easy for any of you ladies.'

'Yup, we all were reuniting after several years, and before we could even catch up and spend time together, Naina was gone. Riya seems to think she took her own life. But that seems so strange. I just don't know what to believe.'

'Hmmm.'

'It's heartbreaking, and now all I can pray for is that she finally finds the peace she couldn't when she was alive.'

'There is something I want to share with you, Maya. I don't know if it's appropriate for me to discuss this with you. But I can tell you were close to Naina.'

'Please go ahead, Dr Arik. What is it?'

'For some reason, I am just as unconvinced that she took her own life. It looks more like an accident or, given the situation surrounding her death, maybe something else.'

'Well, I had thought the same at first, but I met a common friend who surprisingly revealed to me that Naina had tried taking her own life a couple of years back. Don't you think people with suicidal tendencies are more prone to dying by their own hand?'

'As you know I am an ob-gyn, not a psychiatrist, so I will leave the emotional analysis be. But I recognise your deceased friend—she visited me in my clinic. She was in the first trimester of her pregnancy and was very anxious about the baby.'

'Naina was pregnant? And was the baby fine?'

'Yes, the baby was absolutely fine. She had experienced some normal first-trimester bleeding that had made her very anxious. I have seen enough expectant mothers to know that this was not an unwanted pregnancy. I don't think she would ever do anything to harm her unborn child. This is why the suicide theory does not make any sense to me.'

'I had no idea Naina was expecting. Had somebody accompanied her to the appointment? The father?'

'No, she had come all alone. The only reason I brought this up with you is that even though this is confidential information for now, after the autopsy, everybody will know. When the cops show up, this is something I will need to bring to their attention. If they need any further clarification, I would be more than willing to speak to them.'

'Yes, of course. Thank you, Dr Arik.'

'No problem. It's quite amazing that we moved into this building a few months back, and yet today was the first time I met Riya. As you know, hers and ours are the only two families living here, aside from an old lady who lives alone. But she generally keeps to herself. I only see her assistant everywhere.'

'First time?'

'Yes, she seems like a very private person. But her husband, Yug, he's a friendly chap. A lot more outgoing than her. Anyway, I better run now. Take care.'

This was news to me. Riya being a recluse and keeping to herself? She had always been a very social and outgoing person, and that's how I have always remembered her. Another shocker was Dr Arik's revelation about Naina's pregnancy. Who was this mystery man she was dating? Did somebody hate her enough to kill her and her unborn child? I cringed at the thought and more at the fact that I knew nothing about my friend or her life.

19

I walked back to Riya's apartment, struggling to process what Dr Arik had shared with me. Somehow, now Naina's desperation to reach me seemed to have more to do with her desire to share news of her pregnancy with me. If Naina was this desperate to have a baby, the last thing she would do is harm herself; didn't that just make sense? I had to find out more. As soon as I reached Riya's apartment, I went straight to my room and closed the door, pacing up and down, trying to gather my thoughts. I had reached a dead end. The fact that Naina had tried overdosing once, her fear and anxiety, led me to believe that she had perhaps just been pushed to the edge and left with no choice but to take her own life. But somehow, that reasoning made no sense now. Especially after talking to Dr Arik. If Naina's death wasn't a suicide, then what was it? It certainly did not look like a premeditated murder. Accidental, maybe? Could Chef Vik have inadvertently added peanuts to Naina's dish and forgotten to mention it? It somehow just did not make sense to me. Why only in hers and not in ours?

I was feeling claustrophobic inside Riya's house. It was a very odd house indeed. When I had boarded that flight to come celebrate Riya's birthday weekend, I thought there would be slight tension given the circumstances under which we all had parted ways, but now I wished for the awkwardness and tension over dealing with the sudden death of a dear friend.

I joined Riya and Sam in the master bedroom. They were chatting about Naina. Riya looked at the clock. 'Guys, it's getting quite late, perhaps we should all get some rest. It's been a long night, and with the authorities coming in tomorrow, it's going to be an even longer day. It looks like the weather will clear up by then.'

'I agree.'

Even though I had gone over to talk to Sam and Riya, we were all under extreme stress, and I did think a little rest would help clear our heads. I was slightly shaken and needed time to compose myself—this could only happen if I was left to myself.

I laid down under the covers. I felt the fresh scent of Egyptian cotton sheets fill my nostrils. My eyes were starting to get heavy when I suddenly saw Naina's face flash before my eyes, and they shot wide open. Who was I kidding? I wasn't going to get any sleep tonight—I had too many unanswered questions swirling in my head. Besides, all the drinking had made my head a little foggy.

I got up from the bed and stepped into the dark foyer. I heard a sound coming from the living room. At first, I thought it was my mind playing tricks on me, and I continued to walk towards the kitchen when I heard it again. I went to the living room and saw a person bent over Naina's body. I wanted to go and find out who it was, but something stopped me. There was a sudden flash of lightning, and I noticed they were wearing a burqa—it was Sam. Maybe she needed privacy to pay her last respects. I saw her get up, but instead of going back to her room, she went to the utility closet, pulled out an umbrella and made her way to the steps leading up to the roof deck. I stayed a couple of steps behind her. There was a small laundry room up there, which I had spotted earlier, where I could hide and safely see the roof deck, through a glass pane. I noticed Sam, in her flowing burqa, teetering on the edge of the roof, and for a moment, I gasped, thinking that she might be ending her life. Instead, I noticed Sam take something out of her pocket and fling it off the railing. She then rushed back downstairs. What had she thrown away?

I noticed a wet footprint on the dry floor and a memory of us teasing Sam about her impossibly small feet bubbled up to the surface. But what I saw was most definitely not hers—it was at least three sizes bigger. Who was this impersonating Sam?

I waited a couple of minutes before heading down. I was just about to enter my room when I heard a soft 'Boo!' in my ear and yelped in fright. I turned around, and it was Parry.

'Are you nuts? You scared the life out of me.'

'Sorry. It's been so stressful that I was just having a little fun. I did not mean to scare you off or anything.'

'I know. I am not sleepy.'

'Neither am I. Want to chat?'

'Sure,' I said, opening the door to my room.

'Do you mind if we talk in my room? Riya is sleeping and she might call out to me if she needs something. I am 24x7 at Riya's beck and call, especially considering what's happened tonight. I would like to be close to her.'

'Okay,' I followed Parry to his room. I was pleasantly surprised when I entered. His room had a monk-like austerity. There was a single bed with a desk and two chairs. The walls were empty, with no paintings or artwork anywhere. I noticed a shoe shelf with a few pairs of sneakers, slippers and a pair of expensive-looking climbing shoes. I wondered how Parry could afford all the expensive footwear, but I knew it wasn't my place or business to speculate.

'Surprised? You expected a gay man to have a more flamboyant room, right? Posters of Lady Gaga and Prince, perhaps? With Mika playing loudly in the background. Though I must admit Mika's "Love Today" is my all-time fave song.'

'Well, talk about stereotypes.' There was something almost likeable about Parry that despite myself, I was finally able to see what Riya valued in him.

We sat down, Parry pulled out a joint and opened his window. He lit it and handed it over to me. I took a few drags of the marijuana and suddenly felt a lot calmer.

'When Riya told me she was hosting this dinner tonight, I had a bad feeling about it. I discouraged her, but she insisted.'

'Discouraged her? Why?'

'Riya has been going through a lot and has cut back on socialising quite a bit; the last thing she needed was to deal with Yug after it's all over,' Parry said.

'Been through what? Riya looks great to me.'

'It's all a façade. Riya is old-school; she will never let people in on how she is actually feeling. But I live with her, and I know the pain she's going through. You remember earlier this evening when I wanted to talk to you about Riya? It was more like I wanted you to intervene and do something.'

'What's wrong?'

'Well, the usual stress of being new parents, I guess. And then, Riya has always been very extravagant in her spending. Yug is going through a rough patch in business and has tightened the purse strings. In fact, at one point, he was even contemplating filing for bankruptcy, but then his rich daddy temporarily bailed him out.'

'Okay. People go through financial hardships all the time, so I can understand it can be overwhelming.'

'Financial hardship is different in Riya's case. Money gave her a sense of confidence, but now, with Yug's parents bailing them out, it's been rough on her. Especially given how they feel about her…'

'Feel about her? As in?'

'They hate her.'

'Hate is a strong word. I don't think anybody can hate Riya.'

'They felt it was a real step down for him to marry someone like her. Now that they had to bail him out, Riya's self-esteem is at an all-time low. So she is selling her diamonds and bags to make ends meet. That can be rough. Parting with that crocodile Birkin was particularly hard on both of us. We cried the whole day. Especially considering the kind of life Riya has lived and is used to. Now when Yug's parents visit, they act like they own the place.'

I had nothing to say. I had been through financial hardship, so for me, giving up on a few Hermes and Dior bags didn't sound like the end of the world.

'Plus, I fear for Riya when Yug finds out.'

'Finds out what?'

'She just loaned Sam a huge sum of money, and Yug will lose it when he gets to know about it,' he whispered conspiratorially.

'Well, it's between them, Parry. We really shouldn't be talking about it.'

'It's not that. You don't understand. Yug—how should I explain it—he uses money as a weapon against Riya. He does not like her making independent decisions, especially when it comes to money. So Riya loaning money to Sam without his permission is going to drive him crazy.'

I knew Sam was going through financial hardship but taking a loan from Riya seemed absurd to me. But I still did not think it was that big a deal. Friends borrowed and loaned money and things all the time. I felt like Parry was making it sound more salacious than it actually was.

'Okay,' I said, simply.

'Which is why it is so strange that Riya is risking so much to give Sam money. I asked her for money a few months back, and she claimed that she had checked with Yug, and he had said no.

She did not lend me money. This was when I was applying for my US visa.'

'Parry, Parry!' I heard Riya call out.

'Long life. I have to run. Please don't mention any of this to Riya.'

He quickly stubbed his joint on the windowsill, popped a few Altoids in his mouth, sprayed on cologne and left the room. Finding myself alone in Parry's room, I couldn't help but look around. I didn't know what to expect, but maybe I would find the answers to who he was and his role in this household. I started with his desk and opened the first drawer. There was nothing but stationery in it. I opened the second drawer, and there was a blue folder. I pulled it out and flipped through it. I noticed it contained profiles of Naina, Sam and me. It was weird because, in the age of social media, I would imagine a Google search would do the job just as well.

I put everything back and stepped out of Parry's room to look for Sam. She had some explaining to do.

20

I knocked gently on Sam's door. There was no response. I noticed the room was empty. From a corner, I saw her raise herself. She was offering namaz. I stood there for a couple of minutes. Once she had finished, she folded her prayer mat.

'Sam.'

She turned around and gave me a slightly embarrassed smile.

'I was trying to be all cool and not too religious, but I guess you caught me in the act.'

'You know I've always been an atheist, but I have respect for people who aren't. Freedom of choice, etc.'

'I missed her so much over the years, and I wanted to call her and I even did, but she never took my call.'

'What are you talking about?'

'I am talking about Naina. I feel like I might have let her down. I wish I had done something for her. Maybe I could have looked for her, hunted her down and just done something for her. The fact she came to the shelter means she must have been in some kind of trouble, and I did nothing. It's just so sad and unbelievable. Life can be so unpredictable.'

I noticed the sadness in her eyes. She looked distraught and was echoing exactly my sentiments. But I had to talk to her about Parry. If Sam was concerned about something, I wanted to know.

'I know, Sam. But we all had no idea, right? Besides, Naina might have had her reasons for keeping us out of her life. People often do drift away after school, so I wouldn't take it personally at all.'

'You are probably right. Maybe I am reading into things too much. I have been personally going through so much stress lately that I don't find it hard to believe that I might just be overreacting.'

'Are you facing any financial hardships, Sam?' I was going over the conversation I had with Parry, earlier, in my head.

'Financial? Yes, I think I told you that Zayn is not working, and all the financial responsibilities are on my shoulders,' Sam said.

'A little birdie told me that you might have borrowed money from Riya.'

Sam started laughing. 'Well let me guess who the carrier of this information is.'

'What's funny?'

'Yes, Riya did give me money, but it was for safekeeping not as a loan or a gift to me.'

'I know it's none of my business, but why did she give you money?'

'She wanted me to keep it safe. She's on the verge of leaving Yug, and these were her personal savings, which she didn't want him to get wind of.

'Well, okay.'

'There is one other thing, Maya. I haven't told anybody this. But I am extremely stressed about something.'

'What?'

Sam peeped out of her room to make sure nobody was listening. She closed the door, came back inside and held my hands.

'Maya, hear me out before you say anything. I have hidden something from all of you. Oh my God, I wish I could just say it. The money Riya gave me ... well, I had put it in a joint account with Zayn, temporarily. It was around hundred thousand dollars. Before I could transfer it to my own savings account, it was gone—all of it. I had no idea until I logged into my account today and discovered that the money is gone. When I confronted Zayn, he said he spent it all on gambling. He thought he could double or triple it for us. And now Riya wants it back. What am I to do?'

'Well, right now is not the right time to bring this up with her, especially with Naina's passing. Maybe you can tell her before you leave? Though I do feel the sooner you come clean, the better.'

'I am so mad at Zayn—he had no right to put me in this situation. I should have never got into it.'

'Riya is quite wealthy. Can't you buy some time? Besides, it's not like you are running away.'

'I can't. She said she needs it urgently. And you know what's really strange about all this? Since the time I have arrived, Riya has not even once mentioned the money. Going by her text messages, one would have thought that she was in urgent need of it.'

'Didn't you bring it up with her?'

'On text, I told her I would transfer it back, but when I realised what Zayn had done, I decided to stay quiet about it, hoping she wouldn't bring it up again until the end of the weekend. I would never pocket someone else's money. Last night, when you saw me and I fibbed about going to the roof deck to pray, I wanted to talk to you and come clean but then at the last minute, I chickened out.'

Strange coincidence that Riya needed her money back just when Parry had decided to relocate to the US. Something wasn't adding up. Parry exercised a lot of influence over her and had clearly been very disturbed by the idea of her having loaned the money to someone else.

Before I could say anything further, we heard Riya enter the room, and I noticed she had changed into a long colourful kaftan and her hair was tied up in a turban. She had collagen eye packs under her eyes. She was giving off a diva vibe. Another one of Parry's curated looks for her, I bet. I still had so many unanswered questions, but they'd have to wait now that Riya had joined us.

'Please excuse my look, guys. But I have been crying nonstop since this happened, and Parry suggested I wear the collagen eye masks before I get humongous bags under my eyes in the morning,' Riya said.

'Bella's sleeping?' Sam asked.

'Yes. The best thing about babies is the abandonment with which they sleep. It's like nothing can wake them at all,' Riya said.

I looked at Sam, and her behaviour was starting to make a lot more sense. We had all been so heavily focused on Naina that we had ignored the elephant in the room that was Riya. It was clear from my conversation with Dr Arik and Parry that Riya was going through some serious issues.

I had been so self-absorbed that I had, not even for a moment, given any thought to how my friends were doing. Sam probably knew what Riya was going through. So even though she overdid the praises, she was likely just being a supportive friend. I knew one thing, for sure. I wasn't going to repeat the same mistake twice. I had let Naina down, but I would not let Riya down.

21

After my exchange with Sam, something was nagging at me. I was uncomfortable about something, and usually, I wasn't completely off the mark. I tried going over the evening, and nothing seemed unusual. We were still hanging out in Sam's room. I noticed she had her eyes closed and was listening to Sufi music on her phone. Riya was fast asleep. I decided to go to the kitchen and get myself a snack. While some people lose their appetites under stress, with me, it was the opposite. I did a lot of stress eating.

I saw Parry and Chef Vik deep in conversation in the kitchen. Things suddenly escalated, and Parry grabbed the young chef by the neck, threatening to kill him. I ran into the kitchen and separated them.

'Guys, what's wrong with you? Stop.'

'He cheated on me, and I just found out,' Vik said.

'Cheated on you? Are you guys dating?' I asked.

'No, we are not. He's making up stories. Please ignore him,' Parry said.

'Don't lie, okay? I have texts to prove it. What you are doing is very wrong,' the chef said.

'Okay, we were dating. Happy? And now we have broken up. Got it? Now buzz off,' Parry said, and with that, he left the room.

Chef Vik burst into tears. I tried consoling him. I went over to the sink to fill a glass of water and handed it to him.

'I don't know why this happens to me every single time. Every time, I get cheated on,' Vik said.

'Well, it happens to the best of us. If it helps, once a cheater always a cheater. You are better off without him.'

'I guess. But tonight, I gave up on a big opportunity to be here,' Vik said.

'What opportunity?'

'There was a sit-down diplomats' dinner at the Italian Embassy and they needed a sous chef. Giada Laurentiis had flown down from the US just for this. It would have been great exposure for me. But I gave it up for this scumbag. And the worst thing is that I am not even getting paid for this shit,' Vik said.

'You're not getting paid?'

'Well, Parry is so far up your friend's ass and wanted to impress her. I, like a fool, agreed because I thought he was in love with me.'

'Well, don't worry about Riya. I have known her for a long time, and she is a fair person. She will compensate you for your hard work.'

'And to top it all, the death…'

'What was the menu that you had planned for tonight?' I asked, changing the subject to distract Vik.

He proudly went over to his backpack and pulled out a MacBook Air. He opened it and showed me a document containing the details of the menu, ingredients, where he purchased them, etc. Chef Vik, even though he was playing pretend chef, was very meticulous and that was impressive.

There were no peanuts anywhere on the menu. Then what had caused Naina's death?

I suddenly heard a sound. I stopped dead in my tracks. It was a familiar whirring sound; it was coming from the coffee maker and was followed by a beep for when the pot of coffee was ready. That was the sound I had heard in the background when the mysterious caller had called on Naina's phone.

One thing was amply clear—Naina had been murdered, and whoever was calling on her phone had been in this house. This could only mean that somebody was lying and would go to any lengths to hide their secret. Worst of all was that they now knew I was in on it, and that meant that my life was in danger. The thought sent a shudder down my spine.

My thoughts were interrupted by a piercing scream. We all rushed towards the source—Chef Vik, Sam, Devi and me. The only person missing was Parry.

'Riya, what's the matter?'

'Parry, I need him. Where he is?' Riya said crying hysterically.

'Devi, can you go get Parry? Riya, calm down. Parry is probably in the restroom or taking a short nap.' Sam knelt by Riya's bedside and started stroking her head. Riya kept sobbing and asking for Parry. I decided that since Sam was watching her, I might as well go look for Parry myself. Devi seemed to be taking forever. I noticed she was standing right outside Riya's bedroom.

'Devi, what took you so long? Did you find Parry?'

'Madam, please follow me.'

Devi led me to the back of the house, where I had hardly been. She opened the door to a walk-in closet-style wine cellar. Parry was sitting on the floor with a Magnum Dom Pérignon, drinking straight from the bottle. I signalled Devi to leave and gently knocked on the glass door. Parry looked up and continued drinking the champagne, listening to some melancholic soundtrack.

'Parry, all good?'

'Oh Maya, come on in. Join me.'

'Riya has been looking all over for you.'

'I know. I heard her shrieking. That's when I decided I needed a little quiet time to myself. A lot has happened tonight, and as much as I adore Riya, she can be extremely needy and oblivious to another person's needs.'

'Yeah, I can imagine the stress you are under.'

'It has been a rough night for us all. On a lighter note, it will be fun to see Yug's expression when he realises I raided his precious wine cellar. The amount of money he spends on collecting fine wines could feed a household for a year. A couple of months back, we had a power outage and had to go down the stairs from the penthouse. Yug—and I am not kidding you—carried a backpack full of fine wines he had purchased on some auction site that he was scared would get spoilt in the oppressive heat of the apartment.'

We both started laughing at the absurdity of the situation, then sat in silence for a couple of minutes.

'Anyway, enough pity partying. Duty calls. I needed a breather, and I got it. Now it's time for me to get back to work.' Parry got up and left. I continued sitting there.

I looked at the immaculately arranged wines stocked on the wall. The whites and reds arranged by region. I noticed that amongst the whites was a red wine. Given the pristine state of the cellar, I felt an urge to correct it. I stood up and pulled out the bottle and saw that instead of wine, there was a piece of paper in it. I pulled it out and noticed there was a blank cheque inside, signed by Yug. A strange place to store it. Could it potentially have something to do with Parry? I placed the cheque back in the empty wine bottle and walked out.

22

'Come on over, Maya. We were just looking at pictures of all of us in New York. The slideshow from before ... we might as well finish it now,' Riya said.

I stood over them, looking at the pictures but not really focusing.

'Naina was beautiful,' Parry said.

'She was,' Sam whispered.

'I don't see Yug in any of these pics.'

'Well, Yug was always busy with school. He barely hung out with us. That's why if it wasn't for you girls, I would have lost my mind in New York,' Riya said.

'You guys look like such a tight group of friends, whatever happened? How did you all lose touch with each other?' he asked.

'I guess, life happened,' Sam said.

Just then, we noticed the lights flicker and it all went dark.

'Oh, my goodness, no electricity. Now, this is crazy,' Riya said.

'Doesn't this remind you of something?' I said.

'Talk about coincidences. Parry, the last time this happened to us was exactly ten years ago when a hurricane hit New York, and all our apartments had a power cut. So we all decided to stick it out together. An adventure of sorts,' Riya said. 'Though we shouldn't have to suffer in the dark now. I wonder why the power backup hasn't kicked in yet.'

'We really did our best back then, didn't we? We lasted all of two days when you decided to move us into a service apartment on the Upper West Side, Riya,' Sam said.

'Where was Naina?' Parry asked.

We were all quiet.

'Well, she wasn't there,' I said.

'Let's just say that wasn't the first time Naina had disappeared from our lives. We were having dinner the first night of the hurricane, and the next morning, when we woke up, Naina was nowhere to be found. We called her and there was no response. A week later, she showed up as if nothing had happened. She looked in great spirits, so we didn't really press her,' Sam explained.

'So Naina had a tendency to take off at will? A life of no accountability? Interesting,' Parry said.

'Will you zip it, Parry? You have no right to pass any judgment on someone who can't defend themselves,' I said.

'Maya is right. We shouldn't talk about Naina this way. Parry, honey, I know you didn't say it with any malice, but let's just drop the subject,' Riya said, trying to placate Parry.

Just then, there was lightning, and the room was flooded with light for a second.

'Let me go get some candles and matches. The storm must have messed with the generator,' Parry said.

'Girls, I am scared of the dark. Can you come sit with me?' Riya said.

'Of course.'

We all sat quietly until Parry came back with the candles.

Suddenly, we were rudely interrupted by a loud crashing sound in the kitchen. I immediately got up and ran towards the kitchen and spotted Chef Vik bent over, looking around for something.

'All well?' I asked.

'Yes, I can't seem to find my cell phone. I am sorry to have made so much noise,' he said.

'Not at all. I was just worried,' I said.

I left the kitchen and returned to where Riya and Sam were sitting. I noticed Parry cradling Riya against his chest. It was almost maternal. Sam was now sitting on the couch with a blank look on her face like she was thousands of miles away. I did not want to interrupt them, so I walked out of the room and through the front door. It was pitch dark outside. Using the light from my phone, I made my way downstairs. I looked up at the roof deck and tried to imagine the direction from which I had seen the burqa-clad figure going towards the edge when they had flung something. It wasn't raining as heavily as before, but visibility was still an issue. I walked around, not knowing what I was looking for. There was really nothing. I was about to turn around and leave when I saw something shining on the ground. It was the pendant I had seen Naina wearing, earlier. What was the significance? Why would someone feel the need to get rid of it? It did not make sense. I placed it in my pocket.

I then realised I was stranded outside. I still didn't know the access code—so much for my sleuthing! Now I was locked out indefinitely. I hoped the lack of power meant the keypad wasn't functioning, but as I walked back to Riya's building, I noticed that the front door had been left open. Somebody had placed a rock to keep it pried open. Maybe a Good Samaritan had seen me venture out. Was it by chance that someone had seen me exiting the building or was I being watched?

23

When I returned to Riya's apartment, there was pin-drop silence. I went to the living room and walked towards Naina's body. I lifted the sheet and looked at her. I wanted to confirm that the necklace I had seen downstairs was actually hers; I saw that she was no longer wearing hers.

'What the hell are you doing here? Have you lost your mind?!' Riya shouted.

'Riya, calm down.'

'Calm down? You are busy fiddling with a corpse in the middle of the night, and you expect me to calm down. How sick is that? Sam! Sam, come here!' Riya screamed.

Sam rushed into the living room, and behind her, I saw Parry and Chef Vik.

'Can we all please say a prayer for Naina's departed soul? It has been nagging me all night that she left us like this, so I had come to pay my respects, and Riya here thought I was being weird,' I lied. I was good at the lying game.

We all assembled around Naina's body, held hands and maintained silence for a couple of minutes. When I opened my eyes, I saw Sam and Riya looking at Naina's body with a strange look on their faces. After our short prayer, we went back to the living room to sit and chat.

'Had any of you heard from Naina in the last couple of years?'

'Nope,' Riya and Sam responded together.

'When in doubt, Google.'

Using Riya's phone, we searched for Naina Kumari. Many Naina Kumaris came up. We tried narrowing the search but were unable to find our Naina. We eventually decided to go on the NYU alumni website. There, we found information about Naina from only five years ago. What had she been up to all this while? We tried looking her up on social media, but as we had guessed, we found nothing at all.

We sat back in silence, dejected. Suddenly, there was yet another crashing sound, and this time, it had come from the bedroom. We immediately ran towards the sound. When we entered the master bedroom, we saw one of the windows had been left open, and since there was a storm raging outside, a photo frame had been knocked off the wall by the wind and crashed on the floor, broken. I went over and lifted the photo frame. It was a picture of Riya and Yug, taken a couple of years back, clearly during happier times. I placed it back on the table. I noticed that among all the family photos, there were none of Bella with Yug. But there were quite a few of Riya with Bella, and I was surprised to see Bella, Riya and Parry in one pic. The man had clearly made himself indispensable to the larger scheme of things.

'How many times have I told you to keep the windows closed, Parry. Don't you get it?' Riya shouted.

'Sorry,' Parry said and started cleaning up. I noticed that Riya behaved in a very entitled and bratty way with him, and he let her get away with it. It was difficult to say what his position in the household really was, but if I was Yug, his intrusion would definitely irk me too.

Riya had said Parry was somewhere between a friend and a nanny. For all of Parry's annoying ways, he did not for a minute get offended or testy with Riya. He had infinite patience with her, and she could get very taxing and exhausting, at times. But I was still suspicious of the influence he exercised over her. All the stress and exhaustion were clearly getting to me. I really wanted to sleep, but my mind was working overtime, and I could just not get myself to switch off. I had recently started cutting back on drinking, but the stress was too much. Drinking had become a necessity for me in my darkest hours. I went discreetly to Riya's bar and grabbed a bottle of alcohol without even looking at the label and snuck into the bathroom. I put the seat down and uncapped it and took a few swigs. I felt the burning liquid go down my throat. I took a few more swigs. The power was still out, and I wanted to sit in the darkness.

I hid the bottle behind the trash can in case I needed to have a drink later. I had this underlying feeling of fear that this nightmare wasn't over. I splashed some cold water on my face. My hands were shaking, but I needed to stay composed in order to uncover the truth. I took a couple of deep breaths and stepped outside. Sam, Riya and Parry were playing cards, so I joined them. Since the power cut, the apartment was starting to get cold. I noticed Parry and Riya were sharing a blanket, and Sam had her own. Even though Parry was gay, his familiarity with Riya was slightly unnerving. I wondered how Yug dealt with it. Could Parry be the main reason for the tension between him and Riya?

I got into Sam's blanket with her.

'Would you like to join us? We could start a fresh game?' Parry asked.

'No, it's fine. I will just sit here and watch.' I needed time to think, and the last thing on my mind was playing cards.

'You know the saying "lucky in cards but unlucky in love?". As much I love winning, I wish I lost in cards. But I never do,' Riya said wistfully.

Sam looked in my direction and frowned slightly. She could smell the alcohol but decided to remain quiet about it. Everybody in college knew that I went off the rails when I had one too many to drink, and if somebody argued with me after that, the outcome would not be good.

I watched them play silently. I saw Riya's phone buzzing. She looked at the phone number and frowned and put the phone away. The phone kept ringing incessantly.

'It's Yug. What should I do?' Riya asked.

'What do you mean?' I asked.

'Do I take his call?' Riya asked.

'Any reason why you shouldn't?' Sam said.

'Well, if I do take his call, I would have to inform him about Naina. And with this raging storm outside, the last thing I want is for Yug to risk life and limb and come rushing back home.'

'You do have a point, Riya. Besides, there is not much we can do until the storm settles anyway. Perhaps you could take his call and not say anything about it,' Sam said.

I did not say anything. I felt the right thing to do would be to let Yug know. After all, the mishap had happened in his own house and a couple of feet away from us lay the body, decomposing. I shuddered thinking about Naina as a corpse. Before I could air my opinion, Riya had answered the call.

'Hello. What is it?' Riya said.

'Are you out of your freaking mind, Riya?!' Yug shouted.

I looked around and Sam looked as taken aback by Yug's tone as me, whereas Parry looked unfazed. He was probably used to it. But I had known Yug, and he had always seemed like a really pleasant guy, so this was a surprise. Riya had the speakerphone on and indicated for us to be quiet.

'I don't think we should talk right now because you are not in your senses,' Riya said.

'Listen, you talk when I want to. You hear me? I pay your bills. The fancy life you have is all because of me. Do you hear me? You were nothing but a small-time hick. I gave you the life you have today. Show some gratitude,' Yug said.

'How many times will I need to thank you, Yug, for this great life you have bestowed upon me?' Riya said.

'Baby, I have told you a million times that business is not doing well. We are on the verge of filing for bankruptcy. I am trying to liquidate our assets to pay off loans. You have to stop spending like this,' Yug said, trying desperately to soften his tone but clearly exhausted and angry.

'Fine,' Riya responded indignantly.

'Also, we can't afford that princess of yours. You need to get rid of his sorry ass soon. I hope you have told him, baby.'

'Where is all this coming from?'

'You have spent one lakh rupees on your dinner tonight, baby. Mummy was so right about you. I should have listened to her when she said you were a gold-digger and you would do me in one day,' Yug said.

Riya hung up and looked Parry in the eye, as both of them started laughing. Yug started calling again. Riya put her phone on silent, looked at us and resumed her card game.

24

After Yug's obnoxious outburst, there was a lightness in the room. It was almost as if the ice had broken. But for some reason, something bothered me about Yug's call. I had the nagging feeling there was something I was missing out on. Anyway, now was not the time to psychoanalyse Yug and Riya.

Riya looked at us and said, 'You know what, whenever I am stressed out, the one thing I love to do is eat spicy Haldiram's bhujia with nimbu pani spiked with vodka and listen to Lata Mangeshkar on loop. He called me a small-time hick, I think I will be just that.'

Riya got up, and Sam leaned over and held her hand to make her sit down.

'Why do you take this, Riya?' Sam asked.

'Because I know no better, and I love him,' she answered dejectedly.

'I felt the same way about Zayn, but now I am ready to move on. It was a difficult decision to make, just like when I made the decision to spend my life with Zayn, I knew I was burning all bridges, and to be fair, so was he, in a way.'

Suddenly, we heard a loud knock on the front door. I was closest so I offered to go get it. It was pitch dark, so it was difficult for me to find my way.

'Hello, who's there?' I asked.

There was no response. I opened it, and there was nobody outside. Maybe it was the wind. Then I noticed somebody standing on the landing and sobbing loudly. I peered to see who it was and found Chef Vik.

'Hello, are you okay? It's me, Maya.'

'Oh, sorry. I just needed a minute to myself, and then I realised I had locked myself out.'

'Vik, don't be this hard on yourself. I think you are jumping the gun. I know what happened tonight was unexpected, but you can't be blamed for it.'

'I know. It's just that I am scared of the consequences.'

'Why don't you tell me what you are scared of? And I mean *really* scared of.'

I noticed him look over my shoulder, and even though he intended to talk, something changed his mind.

'There's really nothing. Thanks for checking in.'

I went back inside. I noticed everybody was where I had left them.

'Who was it?' Riya asked.

'Nobody. The wind,' I said.

I was finding it really hard to place the motive for the crime. Why did somebody want to kill Naina? The biggest revelation for me this weekend had been the involvement of the so-called mystery man who kept showing up in every aspect of Naina's life. Who was he? Where was he? How could I find him? I knew the answer lay in my pocket. I decided to dial the number using Naina's phone and the hidden SIM card. The phone started ringing. I was getting close.

25

'How ironic that Naina should die tonight,' Riya said, looking out of the window.

'What do you mean?' Parry asked.

'Well, lightning was on Naina's family crest, and there is a storm outside,' Riya said.

'Crest?'

Then it struck me that the pendant Naina was wearing was a bolt of lightning. The question now was, why would somebody want to throw it away?

'Well, Naina belonged to a small princely state. She never liked talking about it, but one drunken evening, we were able to pry out this information from her. They had a palace and all … the works. Looking at Naina, you could never have imagined. She was always so low-key,' Sam said.

'How exotic. She was quite the mysterious woman, wasn't she?' Parry said.

'Well, I don't know about mysterious, but she was certainly weak. All the pampering and overprotection had made her incapable of handling life outside of palace walls,' Sam said.

'Don't you think that's a harsh thing to say, Sam? Naina did not exactly have it that easy. Like all of us, she too had to work hard,' I said.

'I have to agree with Sam. It did make her weak. Why else would she take her own life like this?' Riya said.

'Do we know for certain she took her life?' I said, hesitant to reveal what Dr Arik had told me.

'What are you alleging, Maya? That Naina was murdered and one of us is the killer?' Riya said, laughing.

'Of course, that's not what I meant.' I covered up quickly as I felt like I had crossed a line. Besides, the last thing I wanted to do was annoy anyone at this juncture. 'Talking about family reminds me, don't you think we should let somebody know of Naina's passing? Do you have her family's contact in Ram Nagar?'

'Well, no. But I bet if we Google it, we might be able to find something,' Sam said.

We searched for Kunwar Singh Ji of Ram Nagar, Naina's father, and could find no phone number other than that of the local police station. Since they were a prominent family of the area, we decided to try our luck and call them.

'Hello,' we heard a sleepy voice on the other end.

'Hello ji, my name is Maya Singh. I am a family friend of Kunwar Singh Ji's. Is there any way of reaching them?'

'Who?'

'Kunwar Singh Ji.'

'He is dead.'

'What about his son?'

'They both are dead.'

'Are you sure?'

'Of course, I am sure. They died in a car crash, a year ago. I have worked at this police station and served Hukum's family for the last thirty years. I personally made security arrangements for the funeral. Who are you, Madam?' He asked.

'I am a friend of Kunwar Singh Ji's daughter's, Naina. My name is Maya.'

'Oh Naina bitiya. What a sweet girl. I saw her last at the funeral. It was so sad to meet under those circumstances,' the man said.

'You met her?' I asked.

'Of course, I did. She came with her husband. What a lovely couple they made.'

This was all news to me. I was getting more surprised by the minute. I looked at Sam and Riya, and they looked as surprised as I did.

'It was so nice of her to come. We last saw her when she was a little girl, and then we saw her twenty years later at the funeral.'

'Oh really?'

'In fact, I even have a photograph with Naina bitiya and her husband,' he said.

My heart was in my mouth. This mystery man was the key to a lot of things. If I could just find out who he was, a lot of questions would be answered.

'Do you have the photo right now?'

'Well, it's on an older phone. I need to charge it.'

'Do you think you could WhatsApp it to me?'

'Whatever for? It's personal.'

'Naina passed away tonight, and I just thought since I don't have a photograph of hers, perhaps it could be used to notify people via newspapers.'

'I am so sorry to hear about Naina bitiya. This family is cursed. Give me your phone number, and I will try sending it to you via WhatsApp.'

'Thank you.' I shared Riya's phone number since I had an international number and hung up the phone.

'Can you imagine Naina was married?!' Sam exclaimed.

'Well, maybe she was dating someone and introduced him as her husband? You know how small towns are and the mentality of people,' Riya said.

We heard a gentle knock on the door.

'Come in,' Riya said.

It was Chef Vik.

'Ms Riya, I was looking for you,' he said.

'Yes?' Riya said.

'Can I speak with you for a minute, in private?'

'I am exhausted and have no energy right now. Can we just speak here? Don't worry about them. Whatever conversation we have stays in this room.'

He entered the room and closed the door behind him. He looked noticeably nervous, glancing again and again at a visibly livid Parry.

'Go ahead and speak up,' Riya said.

'I hid something from you,' he said.

'What?'

'I never went to culinary school. I learned how to speak English when I worked at a call centre not too far from here, and as far as cooking is concerned, I have only watched hours and hours of MasterChef. I do love cooking, except I am not the chef I claimed to be. I am just a struggling actor who loves to cook. My dream is to be an actor. Having said that, I cook on the side to make a living. But my speciality is dhaba fare, not this fancy stuff. I just did this as a favour to Parry. It was a last-minute thing, and he really wanted to make your day special, so please don't blame him either.'

'Personally, I don't care. Parry hired you, and last I checked, I am not paying you anything. We barely had a chance to enjoy the meal either, so in the future, if you are looking for a referral or something, that isn't happening.'

'Okay.'

'Is there something else bothering you?' I asked.

'Well, I don't know how to say it. I am no coroner, but Ms Naina passed away right after she consumed the food I made—I just don't want to be held responsible for her death in any way. All I did was collect pre-packaged food from a restaurant in the Diplomatic Enclave in Delhi. The chef is a friend of mine, and he sent me photographs and instructions on how to do the plating. I had nothing to do with the cooking or the preparation, but I can assure you one thing. There were no peanuts in the food,' Chef Vik answered.

26

Parry was in a tizzy, trying to explain his actions, 'Riya, I had no idea about Chef Vik and his credentials. He looked good, so I hired him. To be fair, I have sampled his food, and he does cook up some pretty delicious meals, even if not what we ate tonight.'

'Don't worry, Parry. Nobody is blaming you. It's really okay. You were only trying to make my day extra special. Besides, we have bigger issues. I am so stressed out. Do you think you could get me a glass of red wine, please?' Riya said.

I once again watched the exchange between them with fascination. They were like two peas in a pod and worked in perfect harmony with each other. Clearly, Parry could do no wrong in Riya's eyes.

At that moment, the lights came on.

'Thank God the power is back. That means things must be returning to order,' Sam said.

'Yes. My God, just look at us. I think we should all freshen up now that the power is back,' Riya said.

We all went back to our rooms. I sat twiddling my thumbs, not knowing what to do. I decided to go up to the roof deck.

There was a canopy there, and a little fresh air might do me some good, I thought. As I stepped out, I heard whispers from Sam's room. I did not want to eavesdrop, but it looked like Sam and Riya were talking about me.

'Have you told her anything?' Riya asked.

'No, I have not. But you do need to realise she is an attorney, and she is not stupid. She will figure things out, eventually. Don't you think coming clean is a good idea?' Sam asked.

'Listen, Sam, we had an agreement. Maya cannot find out at any cost, and that's that.'

'I know, Riya, but things have changed. We should tell Maya. She will help us.'

'An agreement is an agreement,' Riya was defiant.

'Fine. Another thing—you let that Parry get to your head too much. It's time to be objective.'

'Unsolicited advice.'

'I will return every penny you have ever given to me, Riya, so you can no longer dangle it as a sword over my head. I was appalled at the message you sent me. You could have just asked me for the cash upfront. You have heard the saying that words once said cannot be taken back.'

'This is not the about the money. What are you talking about? What text?'

'Not about the money? The hundred thousand dollars you transferred to me last week. Did you not send me a text demanding it back? It's your money, you gave it willingly to me. I am not running away with it. So stop acting like you did me the hugest favour. In fact, I did you the favour here.'

'Are you off your rockers? I do recollect transferring the money to you, but I don't remember asking you to return it to me.'

'For heaven's sake, Riya, stop lying. You sent me a text.'

'Sam, I am turning forty, not eighty. I would remember such a thing.'

I had heard enough. I turned around and saw Parry lurking in the hallway. He caught my eye.

'Can I get you anything?' he asked.

'Oh, nothing. I wanted to speak with the girls, but they seemed to be deep in conversation. So I was waiting for them to finish,' I said.

'Okay,' he smiled.

I knew everybody was busy, so this was the right time to go and speak to Devi.

Riya's house was very unusual. It had all the worldly comforts but lacked warmth. I wanted to understand desperately what had been going on. Talking to Devi might not be a bad idea to understand family dynamics.

I found her in the kitchen. 'Devi, can I talk to you? I need to ask you a few questions. I will be quick,' I said.

Devi looked around nervously. 'Riya Madam gets very upset if I stand around talking.'

'Don't you think Riya Madam would get more upset if she knew exactly what you were up to?' I decided to threaten her so she would start talking out of fear.

'You wouldn't tell her, would you?' Devi asked.

And bingo, it had worked.

'I won't if you just answer a few questions.'

'Can we talk in my room, Madamji? That way even if Riya Madam comes looking for me, she will think I have gone to the bathroom.'

'Of course. Any place you're comfortable.'

Once we were settled in her room, Devi asked, 'What would you like to know?'

'How long have you been working for Riya?'

'Madamji, around six months. I came immediately after Bella Baby's birth.'

'You must be so close to her.'

'Yes, of course. I have three children of my own whom I haven't seen in the longest time, and I miss them terribly. They have probably forgotten their mummy by now.' She sounded melancholic.

'Why don't you bring them here?'

'Madam doesn't allow.'

'Okay. Why don't you ask Yug Sir?'

'Sir is never around. But he is the kindest person. Madam was also very nice until Parry Sir moved in. He controls everything now, and Madam doesn't say anything to him. He can get away with anything,' Devi said.

This was interesting. I knew Parry had a lot of influence over Riya, so I wasn't surprised at all that he ran the show. 'I am sorry to hear about Naina Madam, she seemed so nice,' Devi added.

'You knew Naina?'

'Oh yes. She came over just a couple of days back. Actually, the day Sam Madam came, she had stopped by,' Devi said.

Was this the conversation Riya and Sam were having? Why did they make it seem like they hadn't met Naina for the longest time? Something transpired between the three of them that I wasn't privy to.

I was starting to get very frustrated. I was so close to finding out more about Naina, yet I was drawing a blank once again. I looked at Devi, and I knew this was all she had to offer.

'Thank you, Devi,' I said dejectedly and got up to leave her room. There was a lot more to this than met the eye, but there seemed to be no way for me to find out what it was.

27

I went looking for Sam and Riya. I saw them in Sam's room, so instead of eavesdropping, this time around, I knocked on the door and pushed it open.

'Ladies, I think we need to talk, and you have some explaining to do.'

'What do you mean?' Sam said.

'I think there is something you are hiding from me. Naina was here, right? She met you both prior to tonight.'

Riya let out a resigned sigh. 'Sam, why don't you just go ahead and tell her? My head is pounding, and I can't deal with any more stress. I will crack up if this goes on.'

'It happened the day I arrived. Naina was at Riya's gate. I saw her talking to the guard. I called out to her, and I am pretty sure she heard me, but she pretended like she hadn't. When I reached upstairs, I asked Riya if Naina had come visiting, and she said she hadn't. We found it odd that she had come all this way and did not even come upstairs to say hi,' Sam explained.

'So why is that top secret? She came over to leave a note for me,' I said.

'She what?'

'She wanted to talk to me and left her phone number with the guard. It's another thing that I couldn't reach her.'

'My head is spinning, and all this is just very mind-boggling. You know guys, I wouldn't mind getting some rest. I am emotionally, mentally and physically tired now,' Riya said.

We then decided the best thing we could all do now was get some rest. It had been a long day. The rain had practically stopped, and the authorities would show up soon. I only hoped the investigation would be concluded before I had to return to New York. There was no way I could extend my trip. I switched off the light and lay down on the bed. So much had happened in the last twenty-four hours since I had arrived in Delhi.

We all retired to our room, and I realised that things were now finally starting to make some sense. This entire weekend had been planned to get rid of Naina. There was something she had done that had won her an enemy. A person who hated her enough to want to kill her. She was not the kind of person who would hurt anyone deliberately, so this kind of hatred towards her seemed way too extreme, but the person who hated her was still in our midst. Which is why whatever it was she wanted to share with me, she was scared somebody would overhear. It was possible she wanted to share with me that she was pregnant. Why would somebody resent her for her happiness like this? We all loved her to bits and could wish no harm upon her. Unless that wasn't the case, and somebody not only wanted to kill Naina but also her unborn child.

Could it have been Sam or Riya? But why? What grievance did Sam or Riya have against Naina? We all hadn't been in touch with Naina for the longest time; it just didn't add up. Sam was too preoccupied with Zayn to be plotting her friend's murder in her spare time. As far as Riya was concerned, she was clearly going through some mental health issues related to postpartum.

Could it be Parry or Chef Vik? They barely knew Naina, so hating her enough to kill her made no sense. Parry was a strange guy, but he didn't seem capable of murder. He was just an opportunist who wanted nobody else to stand in his way. That left me with Chef Vik, who was just trying to make it big by hook or by crook. So many people did that, except that he was unfortunate enough to have got caught before anything came of it.

The only person left now was Devi. But she seemed like an unlikely suspect as she was the only one trying to help me out. I thought about the EpiPen incident—could it all have been a cover-up to throw me off? It felt like I didn't have all the pieces of the puzzle.

I had reached a dead end. Nobody seemed to have a strong enough motive to do it. The key piece seemed to be the mystery man Naina was dating who we knew almost nothing about. My thoughts went back to the conversation Sam and Riya were having in private. Did they know about him? Was that the secret they did not want to share with me? But why? Now secrets made no difference at all. Naina was gone. I closed my eyes to think. I had to detach myself from all this and let the cops do their job when they got here. I had a tendency to get very involved, and the prudent thing for me to do would be to back off. But I felt like the answers were staring me in the face, and I just had to think a little harder and out of the box. I put myself in Naina's shoes for a moment. If I was attending a reunion with friends who I hadn't seen in years, what would I be most excited about? Seeing them, right? But that wasn't the case—she was scared about something. Besides, if she was really excited to see us, why didn't she straightaway tell us about her pregnancy?

My thoughts were interrupted by a sound. My eyes immediately shot wide open. I saw the door handle to my bedroom being turned. I had kept my door locked since I had stopped feeling safe in Riya's house a while ago. I slipped into my shoes and quietly approached the door. I peered outside, but there was nobody in the hallway. I looked further down and saw some movement. I decided to find out who it was, praying I would not come to regret my decision.

I soon realised it was Devi. I had reached a dead end, and the only way I could uncover the truth was to follow Devi. She was my last hope.

I reached the front door and noticed it had been left slightly ajar by Devi. I followed her down the stairs. A couple of minutes later, we reached the dark basement parking. I was always creeped out by basements. I continued following her to the far right end of the basement. I noticed there were a bunch of doors to what looked like storage units. Suddenly, I could no longer see her. I was standing right in the centre, and there was a killer at large in the apartment complex. Anything could happen to me. I broke into a sweat and was just about to turn around and leave when I spotted a faint light coming from inside one of the storage units. I gingerly made my way towards the light. Entering the storage unit, I noticed the light was coming from a battery-operated electric lamp. I picked it up and looked around. There were boxes labelled 'Riya Sharma' and 'Yug Sharma'. I poked and prodded a few of them, and there seemed to be nothing out of place. I walked towards the back of the storage unit and heard the door close behind me. I ran back in panic, but I had been locked inside. I was starting to get a little claustrophobic and felt like I wanted to throw up. There was old and discarded stuff sitting in the unit, but there was also a rancid smell as if a dead animal was trapped in there. I needed to get out of there.

I looked around for an exit and felt a draught come in from somewhere. I went towards it and removed a few boxes. I still couldn't quite figure out why Devi had guided me here. I opened a few boxes to see if I'd been led here on purpose to find something specific. One contained old shoes, clothes and other knick-knacks. Mostly junk. Maybe I was just wasting my time, and the purpose was Devi wanted nothing then to lock me up. I noticed a bright pink box; unlike the other old boxes, this one was shiny and new. I went over and opened it. I saw a photograph, a lock of hair, a pendant, some school reports and a rotten baby tooth. I glanced at the photographs and couldn't tell who the people in them were. Until I saw one photograph and stopped in my tracks. Suddenly, things started making sense. I had uncovered a very big secret, and I knew it had a connection to Naina's death. I took the photograph and placed it in my back pocket. Now I just needed to find a way out. My heart started palpitating. It was all a lot murkier than I could have imagined.

I heard a low buzzing sound. I was wondering where it was coming from. I removed a few boxes and saw an old, long commercial chest freezer. I placed my hand on it and could feel the gentle vibration and a humming sound. I found it odd that in an otherwise neglected storeroom, there was a running refrigerator. I placed my phone back in my pocket and pulled up the lid of the freezer. I couldn't see what was inside, so I pulled out my phone and turned on the flashlight.

From inside it, Yug's dead eyes stared back at me. I sprang back, the lid shutting with a dull thud. I stumbled on a few boxes that made a loud crashing sound. My heart was pounding, and I was sweating. I needed to look inside to know how he'd died. I lifted the lid once again and noticed that he had been shot in the head. Rigor mortis had set in, and his skin had turned dark purple. I could tell that a couple of hours had elapsed since Yug had been killed. I was about to throw up, so I hurriedly closed the lid. Devi had led me here because she knew all along that he had been killed. This is why I had seen her running out of the building in the middle of the night, even though she had denied it.

I stood rooted to the spot, not knowing what to do for a couple of minutes until I gradually realised I needed to get it together and figure out an exit. I needed to find the killer and save not just my own life, but others' too. I noticed an air vent; if I pushed hard enough, I would be able to crawl out. I tried and after a couple of tries, the vent gave way, and I squeezed my way out of the storage unit. I waited a couple of minutes to catch my breath and compose myself. There was something very sinister going on. But one thing was clear—Yug and Naina's deaths were connected. It was no coincidence that they both had been killed on the same night. Why did anybody want to kill them both? I did a few breathing exercises to calm myself down—I had just seen two dead bodies in one night. It was overwhelming and too much to handle. But I also knew this was not the time to let my nerves get the better of me. I was very close to finding out the truth. With a new resolve, I went back upstairs.

28

When I entered Riya's apartment, I was relieved that there was nobody around. I went straight to my room and locked the door; I placed a chair by the door. I opened the closets and searched the bathroom to ensure nobody was hiding there. I was very scared. I went and emptied my handbag to check that my passport was still there. Thankfully, it was. I took it out and kept it in my pocket—the only place I trusted was safe any more. I couldn't wait to board my flight back to JFK and put this hellish weekend behind me.

I couldn't get the image of Yug out of my head. There was no point looking for Devi. I was pretty sure she was on her way somewhere by now, considering the bus ticket I had seen earlier in her room. I also knew for a fact that she was the one who had locked me up in the storage unit. I was shaking with fear, but I knew I had to bring Naina and Yug's killer to justice. But I needed some time to think first, to make sense of all the facts.

How long had Yug been dead? I remembered his phone call. There was something that had seemed a little off, but what was it? What if it wasn't Yug at all who had called? Riya was way too drunk anyway, so maybe she couldn't tell the difference?

I sat down and fired up my laptop. Naina's death suddenly seemed planned and seamlessly executed to make it look like an accident or suicide. But Yug? That didn't fit in with the rest of the puzzle as neatly. I Googled Sam and went through her LinkedIn page, then her non-profit's.

I Googled Riya and found her Instagram page, which hadn't been updated in a year. It was almost like she had gone underground. A year back, I saw pics of her and immediately recalled the vivacious, social Riya we all knew.

I next searched for Parry. His Facebook page had a picture of mountains as its display photo, and on his Instagram, he posted very generic stuff, mostly related to fashion. I scrolled some more, and it looked like Parry was also interested in free solo climbing. The climbing shoes in Parry's room I had spotted earlier now made sense.

The only person left now was Chef Vik. His Instagram page was filled with provocative selfies. I was getting an Enrique Iglesias vibe. I noticed that he had a bunch of acting clips. I clicked on a few and saw he was immensely talented. I also noticed one thing that was common in all his clips was that he had a special talent for imitating voices. Was it possible that he had impersonated Yug and called Riya before? It did seem plausible now. The only issue with all my inferences was that I had no solid evidence to prove who the killer was, except for my instincts.

My thoughts were interrupted by a baby crying. Bella must have sensed the tension in the house and was reacting to it. Riya had so much to drink that she was probably passed out. Besides, after what I had seen in the storage room, Riya wouldn't be sleeping for some time when she found out. I waited for a couple of minutes, but nobody came to pacify Bella. Then I remembered Devi was in charge and had taken off. I opened my bedroom door and went into Bella's room. I wore the mask and gloves by the door and gently closed the door behind me, so as not to alarm her further.

I quietly stepped into the centre of the room, where the crib was. I saw that the baby was fast asleep, but something seemed a little strange about her. She seemed unusually still. I leaned over and placed my finger gently under her nose to see if she was breathing and found that she was not. My thoughts immediately went to Riya. First Naina, then Yug, and now God forbid if something happened to Bella, I was pretty sure Riya would be inconsolable. I bent down and lifted Bella from the crib and immediately knew what was wrong with her. I almost dropped her in shock and started inching away from the crib. Bella was not a human baby but a doll. She looked so lifelike.

Once the initial shock of my discovery had worn off, I recalled having heard of such dolls. They were called 'reborn dolls'. In the US, reborn dolls were so advanced that one could get them custom-made with human hair, and from a distance, they could be confused with real babies. As far as I knew, they were used to help people overcome the loss of a child or treat related mental illnesses.

I was shocked. Was Riya that unwell? I always knew she wanted a baby, but this was a whole other extreme. I felt sorry for her; she seemed so invested in Bella. It all started to add up. Riya's reclusiveness that Dr Arik had mentioned made sense because it coincided with the time Bella had entered her life. That was the reason why Yug was not interested in Bella and there were hardly any photographs of them together. One thing was clear—Riya needed professional help. I was surprised nobody was giving it to her. I sat on the ground soaking up the extent of the charade.

I noticed that the life-sized teddy bear by the wall had a twinkling light, which I was pretty sure was a hidden camera. Before I was discovered, I had to leave. I did a quick sweep through the room to ensure I wasn't missing anything. It was amazing how the room was equipped with every conceivable product for a baby when there wasn't even a baby. I even noticed a diaper pail, which was extraordinary. I opened it and saw folded diapers. I opened one and found a shrimp ceviche golgappa in it, except that this one had enough crushed peanuts for them to be smelled from a distance.

There was no doubt now that Naina had been murdered. Who could have wanted her dead this badly? I think I was starting to get an idea. I placed the diaper back in the pail and left the room. I was shaking after what I had just witnessed in Bella's room. The killer clearly wasn't going to stop at anything.

29

I was sure now that I had no more time to waste. I walked into the living room and saw Riya's phone lying there. I was wondering if the constable at Ram Nagar had sent over the photograph. Her phone was not password-protected, thankfully, and I could easily get into it. I went straight to her WhatsApp, to a message from an unsaved phone number. I clicked on it and was greeted by a smiling photograph of Yug and Naina. It had been Yug all along!

Yug was the mystery man. The tension in Riya and Yug's marriage now made sense. He was with Riya only because of financial reasons. He had put all his assets in Riya's name to avoid filing for bankruptcy, as Sam had told me. He didn't love Riya. He loved Naina. What he could never have imagined was the wrath of a woman scorned. Riya was out to seek revenge. I was pretty sure that Riya had orchestrated this entire weekend just so that she could get to the bottom of things. I then went to her deleted messages, and there was the text that Riya claimed she had never sent to Sam, asking for the money back.

'Drop that phone,' Parry's voice seemed different. It was no longer light and fun. It sent a shudder down my spine.

Parry was breathing heavily on my neck.

'If you so much as make a sound, I will finish you. You hear me?' I felt a blade on my back. I nodded and remained rooted to the spot. Parry guided me towards a chair and instructed me to sit down. He pulled out a rope and tied my feet and hands. He then took a blanket and draped it over me, so no one could see the ropes.

I was stunned to see Parry's appearance. He was wearing a bob-cut wig and had garish make-up on. His outfit was even more outrageous—he was wearing a sequined, nude body suit with nude Louboutin heels. If my eyes weren't deceiving me, Parry looked like a distorted male version of Riya. I got a sinking feeling in the pit of my stomach looking at him. I think he sensed me looking at him agape. The situation got even more bizarre when Parry started singing.

'You're just too good to be true/ Can't take my eyes off you...'

Parry continued to hum Frankie Valli's famous song.

'Parry, what are you doing?' I had to ask.

'Not a word, you hear me? You squeak and I will finish you all.'

'The way you finished Yug and Naina?' The pieces had finally fallen into place. It wasn't Riya who had murdered them. She was unstable and needed help, but she wasn't capable of violence. Parry, on the other hand, looked absolutely unhinged; a man unafraid of anyone and anything.

'Oh, you are smarter than I thought. Did my warnings have no effect on you? I really did not want to hurt you, but you have left me with no option. It's just that you know too much, darlin'. Stop the charade, Maya— you don't think I know that you knew all along about Naina and Yug being an item?'

I remained silent. I wanted Parry to keep talking.

'Which is why I was shocked at the way you were acting all ignorant,' he said.

'How do you know all of this? Does Riya know?'

'Does Riya know?' Parry mimicked me in a sing-song style. 'Of course, she does. How thick are you, really? And you call yourself a lawyer!'

'When did she tell you?'

'Listen, I know everything about Riya and what I don't know, I make it my business to find out. What's hilarious here is that Riya too knows that you knew about Yug and Naina's affair, yet you decided not to mention it to her.'

'Parry, I really had no idea who the mystery man in Naina's life was until a few minutes ago.' I knew Parry was unconvinced, but it was the truth. The photograph from Ram Nagar was the first time I got wind of Yug and Naina's relationship, but since I was close to Naina, I couldn't blame Parry, or for that matter, even Riya, believing that I knew about it all along.

I started wracking my brain to consider how Riya could have found out about Yug and Naina.

'Did you not think the honourable thing for you to do was to mention it to Riya?' Parry asked.

'Parry, I really did not have any idea. You just have to take my word for it.'

'Excuses, excuses, excuses. I am sick and tired of all of you.'

I was about to respond when Sam and Riya entered the room. Parry put his fingers to his lips to indicate that I remain quiet.

'Hey Parry, what's going on?' Riya asked.

'Maya here was feeling cold so I was just making her comfortable. Come on in, girls. Join us.'

'Hey Cheffy, you join us too,' Parry said cheerfully.

Chef Vik walked inside and Parry went to the door and locked it.

'Why are you locking the door, Parry? What if Bella cries? I won't be able to hear her,' Riya said.

I looked at Riya sympathetically. She was living a lie.

'If she cries, we have the baby monitor, right? It will go off. Don't worry, I have taken care of everything, just like I always do. You just sit back and relax.'

'But I still don't understand; why lock the door?'

'Riya, honey, I'd focus more on the state in which you are. It's your job to always look fabulous, remember? In a bit, I will fix you up. But first, I need to take care of some things.'

Parry said the last bit while looking me straight in the eye. Somehow, all my fear had evaporated, and it was empowering to know I could let the truth out in the open any time I wanted. I had finally found the strength I had been searching deep within for.

'Vik, we all know now that you aren't a chef. But I do know you can fix us some mean drinks. How about you bring us a round of something special? I am in a celebratory mood today,' Parry said, interrupting my thoughts.

'Parry, have you lost your mind? Naina is lying dead in the next room, and you are in a celebratory mood?' Riya asked.

Parry was most definitely insane. I moved a little, and the blanket got displaced. Sam caught my eye, and I signalled to her to remain quiet. I could see the horror on her face. Chef Vik spun around with a cocktail he had prepared, but when he saw me tied up, the glass slipped out of his hand and crashed to the ground.

'Now, now, you know how much I hate a mess, Cheffy. Go get a mop and clean up. Quickly, please.'

Riya glanced at me and her eyes widened. 'My God, Maya. Why are you tied up? Parry, go help her.'

Parry stood still.

'Why aren't you listening to me, Parry?'

'Because I don't like her, and I want her to stay tied up,' he answered flatly.

I couldn't keep quiet any longer. I knew people like Parry, and if Riya pushed his buttons any further, he would explode, and I would become his first target. I had to ensure Naina got justice, and that could only happen if I stayed alive.

'Parry, do you want to share with all of us how you killed Yug?'

30

'What? Yug? Killed?!' Riya screamed.

'Yes. Your precious Yug, who hated and detested you, I killed him. It was not planned, but I did it anyway. Besides, now that I think of it, we get to keep his life insurance money. The penniless miser did leave us something in the end after all.'

'What did you do to him, and when did you even kill him? You are lying! I just spoke to him an hour ago,' Riya was now holding Parry by the collar and shaking him.

'It wasn't Yug you spoke to Riya. You spoke to Vik impersonating Yug. And what an Oscar-worthy performance!' I said.

'You are lying to me, Maya. It was Yug,' Riya said.

'Remember, Riya, Yug would get really annoyed when you referred to him as "jaanu", "honey", "baby". He hated such nicknames. But the Yug who called earlier tonight kept calling you "baby". I found that unusual as he was clearly mad at you, so why was he constantly using a term of endearment? Also, there was a whirring sound in the background. It sounded very familiar, and when I connected the dots, I discovered it was your coffee maker. I have the same Smeg coffee maker. Mine only beeps a couple of times to indicate when the coffee is done, but yours is faulty so it made a strange whirring sound and kept beeping incessantly. So whoever was calling was calling from inside the apartment. That was when I knew something wasn't right, and the person calling you wasn't Yug.'

'But did you hate Yug so much that you took his life?! Didn't you for a minute think what it would do to me? That it would destroy me?' Riya asked him, completely ignoring what I had just said.

'I hated him because he took you away from me. I hated the way he treated you, and you kept taking it, day after day after day. He humiliated you and treated you so badly. He cheated on you, and you just kept taking it. That's why I killed him and his precious Naina,' Parry said.

Sam crept closer to me and began quietly untying the ropes that bound me as Parry and Riya got into a screaming match.

'I know, but I cheated on Yug too. I never told him about you. Besides, Parry, you know very well why I was putting up with him. It was only because of you,' Riya said.

'Do you think I cared after all that I had been through? You know, when I was a child, I was confused. I lived with a lady who only took me in because society expected her to be a mother when she had no interest in me, and her husband beat me up whenever he got the chance. The only time I got excited and had something to look forward to was when you came into my life. You were the only bright spot in my life.'

'I know, Parry. But I was doing all this to give *you* a good life.'

'You call having an abusive and neglected childhood a good life? If you hadn't paid the school fees directly to the school, they probably wouldn't have even educated me. And boy, I hoped my nightmare would end in my childhood. But then I hit puberty, and I started getting this strange feeling that I didn't belong in this world. Worst of all, I couldn't even talk to anybody.'

'Parry, I have apologised a million times for doing that to you.'

'It doesn't matter. At first, I was excited you had finally accepted me and wanted me to live here with you, but I was a misfit from day one. I saw how that man, Yug, treated you. He wasn't even in love with you. I don't even think he ever loved you. And it was all because of Naina. She had ruined not just your life, but mine too. This is why I hatched this weekend plan so you could confront Naina once and for all and get some closure. I could not bear to live with a mentally ill mother any longer.'

31

'Mother?' Sam said, reeling in shock.

I pulled out the photograph from my back pocket and threw it on the ground. The baby keepsake box I had found in the storage was Parry's stuff as a baby whom Riya had given up for adoption. I could see the look of astonishment on Sam's face.

'It is true. Parry is my son, and I failed him like I failed Yug,' Riya said, sitting down dejectedly.

Suddenly, she looked haggard and a lot older.

'Will you please tell us what happened now?' I said.

'I was sixteen years old. I fell in love and got pregnant. My parents sent me away to have the baby. Once Parry was born, I gave him to a childless uncle and aunt so they would raise him. But whichever part of the world I was in, at some level, I felt like I had let him down. A mother is a mother. So I started working as an air hostess, and a chunk of the money I made, I paid towards Parry's upbringing. And then I met Yug. He was way beyond my league but also my ticket to a better life. We started dating and quickly got married. I never told him about Parry. But then I suffered a few miscarriages and felt like karma had a role to play. How could God bless me with a child when I had abandoned the one I had? So I hatched a plan for Parry to come live with us. He saved my life.'

'Was the reborn doll his idea?' I asked gently.

'I was going through an emotionally tumultuous time, and Parry introduced me to Bella and reborn dolls, and that was all the therapy I needed, it seemed. Once Bella came into our lives, Yug wanted to have nothing to do with me,' Riya said.

'Bella is a doll? Not a real baby?!' Sam asked. 'This is all so perplexing—didn't the doll, I mean Bella, cry?' Sam said.

'It was recording set on a timer,' said Riya, finally sounding clear and lucid. 'I couldn't cope with being childless. So Parry ordered this doll from the US for me. At first, I thought it was a ridiculous idea. But gradually, Parry started encouraging me to go shopping and buy baby stuff. We set up a mock baby registry, and Parry pretended to be a friend or uncle and routinely bought me a bunch of stuff. We started decorating the nursery, and I had never felt happier. I was so immersed in the bliss that I did not feel the need to leave my house any more. I had everything I had ever wanted under one roof. Except for Yug. He was never mine. But I knew that I couldn't live with my in-laws and maintain the lie. So when the opportunity to move into this secluded apartment complex raised its head, I pounced on it and convinced Yug to move, too. That was when Parry and Bella joined us here,' she explained.

'How did you find out about Yug and Naina?' Sam asked.

'On graduation night, I saw them together. I overheard Yug talking to someone, and when I followed him, I saw him meeting Naina. I was obviously heartbroken, and I didn't know what to do. So I waited for them to finish talking. After he left her, I stood outside the apartment she lived in with you girls and approached her. I confronted her about her affair with Yug. She started crying, and I lied and told her that I was pregnant. Naina was under the impression that Yug and my relationship was over, which was true, but I lied anyway because I was desperate to hold on to him.'

'This is all so baffling,' Sam said.

'Naina couldn't envision a life without Yug and my so-called pregnancy convinced her she had lost him forever. She had Yug's number on her phone, so when he got a call from the hospital on the night she overdosed, he went to get her. I overheard them talking, and Naina told Yug clearly that she wanted to have nothing to do with him, after which he came back home,' Riya said.

'When did they resume their affair?' Sam asked.

'Well, Yug and I were mismatched from the get-go. Unfortunately, my being childless contributed to it. So when he met Naina again, it was love at first sight. They were like two peas in a pod. Given Yug's fancy private school education and her high upbringing, they were made for each other. Initially, I thought his love for Naina was just a phase. But it turns out he had always been in love with her and her alone. Ten years later, she still had him in a way I never could. But as luck would have it, he had to live with me because by then, he had transferred enough assets and money in my name for tax reasons to be tied to me. I threatened to not give him a penny if he left me,' Riya admitted, tearily.

'Which is why I took care of both of them for you, Mommy dearest. Now it's just the two of us with so much wealth, we will never have to work again our entire lives,' Parry said.

'Parry, stop talking before I strangle you,' Riya shouted. Parry looked at her and started laughing.

'Did you plot this?' Sam asked.

'No, I did not. I only planned to kill Naina. But unfortunately, I couldn't rein in my temper. I had a vicious altercation with Yug in the car park, which is why I had to kill him too. This is where Miss Perfect, I mean Maya, comes in. I knew that she would not remain quiet and would poke around until she had discovered the truth about Naina. So I tried different ways to scare her off. But boy, is she tenacious or what?! She went and spoke to that stupid doctor, who revealed to her that Naina was pregnant,' Parry said.

'Oh my goodness. Naina was pregnant?! That's really sad. Riya, did you know?' Sam said.

'Of course, she did. I told her. Naina's business had become my business. How do you think Mommy, who was headed for the loony bin, was convinced to host this weekend of indulgence for her worthless, thankless friends? It was to settle scores. Each one of you has wronged Riya in one way or another. Especially this one,' Parry wagged his finger at me.

'Yes, Maya. I was shocked. You knew everything, and yet you couldn't think beyond Naina and how she was doing. Fine, you guys were close, but she was breaking up my marriage, and you didn't even bother to tell me?' Riya said.

'Riya, you know that's not true. I had no idea until now. The only thing I knew was there was a man in Naina's life, and he was wreaking havoc on her. But not even in my wildest dreams could I have imagined that man was Yug,' I said, trying to restore calm. It was only a matter of time before Parry did something to endanger all our lives.

'You see how worthless she is, Riya? Even now, after she's heard everything, she's still siding with Naina and lying to you. The woman who was responsible for destroying our lives. Which is why from the moment Maya came, I knew I had to set her right,' Parry said.

'You know that's not true, Parry. Keep your toxicity to yourself. But I still can't somehow fathom that Naina and Yug were having an affair. I mean Riya, in not so many words, had indicated that she and Yug were having issues, but I couldn't possibly have imagined one of us being responsible for their domestic discord,' Sam said.

'Parry, why did you have to kill Yug, though? Why? You know we could have worked things out. I had finally got him onboard with the idea of going for couples therapy. And now I've lost him forever… I am nothing without Yug,' Riya said.

'This is what I hate about you. The false sense of loyalty and self-righteousness you have for a man who has caused you nothing but pain. Do you hear me? Pain! Don't you see it? I *had* to take care of him, once and for all, and that's that. Since you are missing him so much, here. Take this.' Parry flung something across the room at Riya. It looked like Yug's thumb.

I peered at it and almost wanted to throw up. Riya leaned over and picked it up. She gasped and collapsed. Sam ran to comfort her.

'This stupid hi-tech building. Most secure places needed Yug's thumbprint. I decided to cut it off to get access to his safe. And who knew it would serve the dual purpose of being a memento for my Mommy dearest here. What an annoying house. But I had to convince Mommy to move. We needed a remote place to set up our lives and finally live in peace.

'Oh, and how can I forget you all? Since you all are witnesses, I will need to set this room on fire and take care of all of you next, so we can put an end to this charade and I can move on with my life,' Parry announced, looking at himself in the mirror and adjusting his wig.

'Do you really think you will get away with this deranged plan of yours, Parry?' I asked.

'I will. I dare you to stop me,' Parry said.

I realised the only way to stop him was to stall him, and to stall, I had to engage with him.

'Why did Naina come for this reunion under such circumstances?' Sam asked.

'Sometimes, we might look for complicated answers when it's really quite simple. Naina was tired of running, and she just wanted to come clean. And what finally gave her the strength to come and talk to Riya and all of us was her unborn child. It was over between Riya and Yug, and he had already decided Naina and he would relocate to the UK,' I said.

'How do you know all this?'

'Because I saw Yug's ticket confirmation on his computer. What's interesting is that there were two tickets booked under Mr and Mrs Sharma. Given the tension between Yug and Riya, there was no way they were travelling anywhere together. Especially since the time overlapped with us being here—Yug was going to leave on the night of Riya's birthday dinner and wait for Naina at the airport. She intended to talk to Riya and all of us, and then head to the airport to join Yug. Except, Naina never made it.'

'Okay, I am bored with your sleuthing, Nancy Drew. Now it's time for me to finish business and meet JJ, the love of my life. Gosh, I would have left earlier but for this Sam stealing all my money. I even forged Yug's signature on a blank cheque without realising he was penniless and there was no money in his account to steal. If things had gone according to plan, I would have killed Naina, made it look like an accident and left. But Yug came back and as usual, ruined my well-laid-out plan,' said Parry.

'What I don't understand is, why were you trying so desperately to stop *me*?' I said. I was running out of questions. I had to keep him engaged. I caught Chef Vik's eye, who was partially crouching behind a couch, hoping that would save him. I signalled to him to distract Parry.

And then I saw Vik holding a gun. Parry was so busy talking, that he failed to notice the gun, so I signalled Vik to pass it to me discreetly. I could tell by the fear on Vik's face that the weapon was useless in his hands anyway.

'It's simple. I saw Naina give that slip to Ravi at the front gate. I approached him and gave him some cash, and then had a look at the note. On it, Naina had written her whole love story for you, Maya, explaining her affair, and more importantly, her reasons for not breaking up, her pregnancy, etc. She had said how she feared for her life and was scared about attending the dinner, but she also felt like the truth had to come out sooner or later. So she wanted to keep you in the loop should anything happen to her. After reading the note, I knew what had to be done. I tore it up and instead wrote down an old phone number of mine, so you would think Naina was calling you to give you some dumb apology. More importantly, if Naina mentioned the note, you wouldn't be surprised,' said Parry.

We all stood there staring at Parry with our mouths open. He had thought of every little thing. He was unstoppable, and we had to act fast before he killed us all.

'Parry, pal, I have nothing to do with all this. Please let me go,' Vik pleaded.

'He's right, why don't you let Sam, Chef Vik and Maya leave? You have a problem with me, settle it with me. But don't harm them, please,' Riya said pleadingly.

'Too little too late, Mommy,' Parry said. 'Now, where did I put that gun?' He began rummaging around the room.

'Parry, please, I beg you. Don't throw your life away like this. Why don't you just leave? We won't complain to the authorities, I promise. As far as the money is concerned, don't worry about it. I will give you as much money as you need and more. Just set us free. By killing us, you will never be able to live in peace, my son,' Riya had gone over to Parry, and they were standing very close to the edge of the big French windows, that were open.

'Leave me alone. Don't touch me and don't call me your son. I hate you. You created this, and now you deal with it,' Parry screamed.

Riya was standing precariously close to the edge of the window, and Parry was not in the right frame of mind. Anything could happen.

'Parry, leave Riya Madam alone,' said Vik, suddenly gathering the courage to point the gun at him. He was shaking with fear.

'Shoot me, you twerp. Go ahead,' Parry said, laughing loudly.

Riya went over and clutched Parry's hand, the one not holding the knife. I got up and raced across the room as he was momentarily distracted by Vik. Parry was caught unawares, and I swiftly pushed Riya aside and tackled Parry, who held the knife a couple of inches away from my stomach. I was on the verge of my guts being spilled out when, out of nowhere, I saw Devi emerge. She had been hiding in a nearby closet all along. With all her strength, she pushed Parry out of the window. He lost his balance and went crashing down. We all stood frozen for a couple of minutes.

Devi looked at me and ran out of the room.

32

'He killed Yug, he killed my Yug…' Riya kept muttering.

We all stood in silence, shocked at how three people had died in just a little over twenty-four hours. It was all too much for us to handle. Suddenly, we heard the doorbell ring. The cops were finally here.

'Is this Ms Riya Sharma's home?' a cop asked.

'Yes, it is.'

'Can we speak with her?'

I looked in Riya's direction; she had a spaced-out look on her face and did not seem like she was in any condition to talk. The cop followed my gaze.

'Is that her?'

'It is, but I think she's in deep shock. If you like, I can answer all your questions. I was present here when the unfortunate events took place.'

'Okay.'

I then described all that had unfolded in detail. I took the cop and showed him where Naina was lying. I then took him downstairs to the storeroom and told them where they could find Yug's body. When we reached the back of the building, Parry was nowhere to be found.

'You mentioned someone by the name of Parry?'

'Yes.'

'Where is he?'

'Well, we pushed him out of the window in self-defence and he fell.'

'Madam, I don't see anybody here. You do realise that no person would be able to survive a fall from that height.'

'You are right, sir. Let me call my friend, Sam. She witnessed Parry's fall too, and so did the chef.'

We went back upstairs. Sam and Vik confirmed that Parry had indeed fallen. So where was his body? He was the main suspect, so a manhunt was launched.

We were questioned for the rest of the day, but there wasn't enough evidence to pin the murders on us, so we were let off the hook. They took Naina and Yug's bodies away, telling us that they would reach out to us if they needed any further testimonies.

'I will never be able to recover from this, Maya,' Sam said, crying.

'Me neither. That's why we need to stick together. Even her,' I said, pointing towards Riya.

'Will she ever get better? The doll… My God,' Sam said.

'The doll is what makes me think Riya will recover,' I said.

'Why is that so?' Sam asked.

'The doll had nothing to do with her having had miscarriages and not being able to procreate or become a mother. She was sixteen when Parry was snatched away from her; he was a newborn. She never got over that. So when she was introduced to the doll, it was like she got a do-over with Parry. She never could've connected with the adult Parry; she likely just felt duty-bound. The doll was her lost baby—not Yug and her baby, just hers.'

'What happens now?'

'She has lost her child in front of her eyes. I think she finally has closure. Now she can grieve for him in peace.'

The next morning, the cops came back. They had a few follow-up questions.

We were taken to separate rooms for the questioning. Dr Arik was also brought in. Chef Vik had been let off the hook.

Riya was devastated about Parry's passing; it was a loss she would never be able to come to terms with. Her only fault had given her a lifetime of sadness. The doll had merely been a coping mechanism. She was clutching onto Bella tightly and swaying back and forth when the cops arrived. A lady cop asked her if she was okay and needed anything, but I could see Riya was in a state of shock, and it would be a while before she became aware of anything again.

All the murders were under investigation, and the police seemed baffled by Parry's missing body. But I was free to return to the United States. Sam was extending her trip by a couple of days to be with Riya. I went over to my room and collected my suitcase and wheeled my bag out of the room. So much had happened in the last couple of days.

Before leaving, I said goodbye to Riya, but she was unable to register my presence. I spoke to Sam and found out that she had made the difficult decision to finally leave Zayn, and I was proud of her. She had also called and spoken to her family, who had long forgiven her for marrying him. They were only waiting for that one phone call, and once she made it, they agreed to meet her. As for Devi, I knew she had taken off on that one-way bus ride.

Even though this had been a heart-wrenching trip, and the losses were far greater than I could ever have imagined, I was glad I came. I always felt Naina and I had parted on unpleasant terms. I had called her the choicest names and abuses without really knowing or understanding where she was coming from. I had lived with that guilt for so long now, and I couldn't even blame her for wanting to cut me out of her life. I looked back at Riya's opulent apartment and realised how one could have everything in the world, and yet nothing at all.

I stepped into the waiting car, which was not a canary yellow SUV. I reached the airport and went through the formalities mechanically. I made my way to a coffee shop and ordered a double shot of espresso for myself. I gulped it down and immediately felt better. When I went to the trash can to throw away my empty cup, that's when I saw it. A crumpled-up bag. I pulled it out and it read 'Riya's 40th'. Parry was alive and somewhere here. Then suddenly, I realised something. I picked up the phone and called Sam and told her exactly what I had discovered. Parry was a rock climber. Since Riya's building was under construction, there were ropes lying about everywhere. When Parry was pushed out of the window, he probably grabbed onto a rope or the scaffolding and made his way down using his skill as a rock climber.

When I boarded my flight, my thoughts immediately went to the crazy weekend I had just had. I was glad to be returning to New York and putting everything behind me. I firmly resolved to do a better job of staying in touch with Sam and Riya. We had all been through so much together—we needed to be there for each other. I looked out of the window and the air stewardess announced our flight was ready for take-off. I closed my eyes for a second, and when I opened them, I noticed they were moist. I then felt a hand lightly tap me on the shoulder and almost jumped. I saw Dhruv sitting on the seat next to me. For a minute, I couldn't believe my eyes.

'Before you freak out, I heard about what happened and got your flight details from Sam. I was to travel to New York for work next week, but I changed my plans as I thought you might need a friend on the fourteen-hour flight back. You went through too much.'

'Thanks, Dhruv, it means a lot.' I took his hand and squeezed it.

I looked out of the window and knew this was Naina's way of playing Cupid.

ABOUT THE AUTHOR

GIRVANI DHYANI is an author, screenwriter and lawyer. She has master's degrees in law from the London School of Economics and Political Science, London, and Cardozo School of Law, New York. She co-wrote the story and screenplay for the movie *Neeyat*, and her first book, *Stalked*, was published in 2014. She lives in Jersey City, New Jersey, with her husband, son and fourteen-year-old French bulldog.